Living Force Campaign G

DESIGN:
ROBERT WIESE, ANDY COLLINS

EDITING:
BRIAN CAMPBELL

LUCAS LICENSING EDITOR:
BEN HARPER

MANAGING EDITOR:
KIM MOHAN

STAR WARS RPG CREATIVE DIRECTOR:
THOMAS M. REID

ART DIRECTOR:
ROBERT RAPER

LUCAS LICENSING ART EDITOR:
IAIN MORRIS

CARTOGRAPHY:
RICK ACHBERGER

TYPESETTING:
ANGELIKA LOKOTZ

COVER ART:
ADI GRANOV

INTERIOR ART:
ADI GRANOV, LUCASFILM LTD.

PROJECT MANAGER:
AMBER FULLERTON

PRODUCTION MANAGER:
CHAS DELONG

SPECIAL THANKS:
MORRIE MULLINS, PETER KIM

www.wizards.com   www.starwars.com

U.S., CANADA,   EUROPEAN HEADQUARTERS
ASIA, PACIFIC, & LATIN AMERICA   Wizards of the Coast, Belgium
Wizards of the Coast, Inc.   P.B. 2031
P.O. Box 707   2600 Berchem
Renton WA 98057-0707   Belgium
(Questions?) 1-800-324-6496   620-T11963   +32-70-23-32-77

Introduction	2
1: Cularin System Overview	**3**
Age of Discovery	3
The Coming of the Jedi	4
The Tarasin Revolt	6
Rise in Crime	6
Trade Wars	6
Cularin Today	7
2: Cularin System Catalog	**7**
Acilarus	7
Cularin	10
Native Species of Cularin	11
Rennokk	19
Tilnes	20
Genarius	22
Ulbasca	31
Ostfrei	32
Uffel	32
Eskaron	35
Asteroid Belt	35
Almas	37
Dorumaa	40
Morjakar	43
3: Power Groups in Cularin	**43**
Metatheran Cartel	43
Caarites and Filordi	44
Organized Crime	45
Military Might	49
Pirates	51
4: Mysterious Places	**51**
Cularin: The Ishkik Caverns	52
Cularin: The Sacred Ch'hala Tree Grove	52
Rennokk: The Cave City	52
Tilnes: Kaernor's Smile	53
Genarius: The Abandoned City of Nub Saar	54
Eskaron: The Worm	55
Asteroids: The Crystal Snare	55
Almas: The Fortress of the Sith	57
5: The Almas Academy	**57**
Curriculum	58
Personalities of the School	59
6: Living Force Campaign Information	**61**
The RPGA Network	61
Living Campaigns	62

Based on the *Star Wars Roleplaying Game* by Andy Collins, Bill Slavicsek, and JD Wiker, utilizing mechanics developed for the new DUNGEONS & DRAGONS® game by Jonathan Tweet, Monte Cook, Skip Williams, Richard Baker, and Peter Adkison

Introduction

A long time ago in a galaxy far, far away . . . .

"I sense a great disturbance in the Force. It comes from the Jedi academy on Almas. I stretch out with my mind into the Cularin system, but I cannot find the source of my distress. It is a haze, a mist that shifts and disperses when I come too close. Somewhere out there, a great evil is growing. Soon it will threaten my students, and possibly even this academy. If we are not prepared, it may threaten much more.

"Cularin attracts a lot of interest from outsiders. Tibanna and irolunn gas, rare woods, ch'hala trees, and various crystals are all valuable commodities here. The Republic government, the Metatheran Trading Cartel, the so-called Smuggler Confederation, and many honest (and dishonest) merchants flock to the system like mynocks to a ship's hull. In their wake come explorers, bounty hunters, fringers hoping to make their fortunes, gamblers, exiled politicians from other systems—everything the galaxy has to offer. The system's main planet, Cularin, serves as a base for many of these interests, as well as a home to the system's native sentient species, the Tarasin. Genarius, a planetary gas giant, harbors huge floating cities that mine gas, manufacture technology, offer gambling, and entice with other entertainment. The asteroid belt hides smugglers, pirates, rogue Jedi, and even a few honest beings who just want privacy. Even the moons hold life, supporting many commercial operations. Unfortunately, with 10 million beings living on the system's three main planets and seven moons, evil finds plenty of places to hide.

"The Force is strong here. The ancient Sith knew this well. A half-buried fortress on the desert side of Almas stands as a mute testament to their interest in the system over a thousand years ago. The Tarasin have a natural ability with the Force that I have only begun to understand. One of the moons provides excellent crystals for lightsabers—the crystals have drawn Jedi here for decades. The natural strength of the Force is the reason my predecessor, Nerra Ziveri, came here to build a new Jedi academy. That, and the need to keep a watchful eye on the Sith fortress. The dark side is strong there, very strong. But I feel the dark side elsewhere in the system, too. Weaker, but still present. It is as if evil has been sleeping here for centuries, ever since the Sith left. Now something, or someone, is stirring it to consciousness.

"The future of this system is hard to see. Even Yoda cannot predict what is to come. I have tried and failed, sometimes investing more effort in worrying about the future than minding the living Force embodied in my students. Yet I must prepare them, and through them, all beings who live here. The coming days will be dark, and difficult to survive. We will need the Force to triumph."

—Jedi Master Lanius Qel-Bertuk

Welcome to Cularin, a system in the Expansion Region of the galaxy. Cularin is located close to the Corellian Run

Trade Route and possesses a variety of resources that attracts the interest of sentient beings from across the galaxy. Gravitic anomalies and gravity shadows make hyperspace travel to Cularin expensive and time-consuming, giving the system a feeling of remoteness in the midst of galactic activity. And, as Master Qel-Bertuk has observed, there is evil present amidst the populace of this burgeoning locale.

Cularin, the home system of the RPGA® Network's Living Force campaign, is a place where adventure thrives. In these pages, you'll find the planets of the Cularin system, systemwide power groups, and insights into the local Jedi academy. Characters abound here: villains, heroes, and the sentients in between who serve the highest bidder. Mysteries and unexplored places abound, all waiting for you.

For information about the RPGA Network and the Living Force campaign, turn to Chapter 6. There you can read instructions for creating characters, find rules specific to the campaign, and see some additional character options for RPGA members. You may find that these new options, and the Living Force adventures, enrich your home campaign as well. You are welcome to use them. Whether you play in the Living campaign or use this material for your home *Star Wars* campaign, the Cularin system offers myriad possibilities for adventure. Enjoy your exploration of this new addition to the *Star Wars* universe, and may the Force be with you.

Cularin System Overview

Aeons pass. . . .

A black hole collapses into itself and disappears, agitating a nearby nebula. The strain on the nebula alters its internal gravity. A star forms in its center, a bright beacon of hope in a muddled cosmic mass. The nebula slowly changes. A thousand millennia later, a second star forms, sibling to the first. The two begin orbiting one another.

Millennia pass. . . .

The nebula spins into a plane and collapses, dispersing and coalescing into a system of five planets. A gas giant shows brief signs of becoming a third star, but falls short, settling into a planetary orbit instead. Its mass attracts a small system of its own that will later flourish within a brilliant gaseous atmosphere. A cloud of comets, born near the edge of the nebula, skirts the fringes of the system.

A rogue planetoid hurtling through space is pulled toward the system. It falls into an eccentric orbit around the two suns. It hides far from their light, but is unable to break away from their grasp.

One of the system's planets is subjected to catastrophic stresses from within. It explodes, sending shock waves and debris through space. Most of the pieces settle into the former planet's orbit, forming an asteroid belt and dividing the system. A few rocky asteroids escape. Two crash into one of the gas giant's moons. The moon becomes highly volcanic and belches dust clouds over its surface.

On the second planet, life evolves. Rain forests and jungles develop around mountains stretching to the clouds. Among the trees, a reptilian race achieves sentience and develops its own society. It lives peacefully, unaware of other worlds for thousands of years, happy to believe the stars above will forever remain beyond its grasp.

Centuries pass. . . .

A man dressed in black steps off a transport. He builds a refuge for himself on the fourth planet, just outside the asteroid belt, where he can delve into the mysteries of the dark side. By creating a form of plant life, he converts the poisonous atmosphere of his chosen world into breathable gas. As it warms the surface of the planet, the world's ecology subtly changes. The figure in black is eventually hunted and forced from the system during the Sith Wars, leaving behind his ecological creation and a grim fortress half buried in the ground. The Jedi who fought him take no note of the system, pleased to have defeated the Sith. They log the system's name, Cularin, in a database and promptly forget about it.

And time passes. . . .

Age of Discovery

An explorer named Reidi Artom emerges from hyperspace at the edge of the comet cloud, warned by her ship's sensors of anomalous gravity wells. Bringing her ship sharply about, she

CULARIN SYSTEM TIMELINE

In the following table, years are expressed relative to the events of *The Phantom Menace*. On Cularin and Almas, years are measured relative to Reidi Artom's discovery of the system (A.A., or "After Artom"). If a character needs to refer to the year of an historical event, add 200 to the number listed on the left-hand side of this table. For instance, the current year in the campaign is 201 A.A.

Year	Event
−200	Reidi Artom "discovers" the system
−175	Artom leaves for the Unknown Regions
−156	Jedi Kibh Jeen turns to the dark side
−149	Kibh Jeen defeated
−145	Jedi Academy established on Almas
−129	Tarasin Revolt begins
−122	Jedi negotiate Cularin Compact and end Tarasin Revolt
−87	Nerra Ziveri assumes charge of the Jedi Academy
−84	Trade Federation achieves control of trade in Cularin
−78	Riboga the Hutt establishes criminal organization
−24	Nerra Ziveri disappears; Lanius Qel-Bertuk becomes Academy Headmaster
−21	Nirama assumes control of criminal and smuggler organizations
−1	Metatheran Cartel formed; trade conflicts begin
0	Trade Federation driven from Cularin system; Neimoidians defeated at Naboo system
1	Living Force campaign begins

comes to a stop and scans the space ahead of her. "Comets. And nothing on my star charts, either. Could be interesting." She smiles a crooked smile. She lives for this sort of discovery. Flying a course around the comet field, she sees a star system ahead of her. A short hyperspace jump brings her into the system. She immediately begins surveying the planets from orbit, one by one.

"A rock. Seen one, seen 'em all. A planet, looks habitable, definitely a thick atmosphere. A gas giant. Need to make sure we check the composition there, see what kind of gases we're dealing with, make sure you can live in them. Probably plenty of room in there. Some kind of outer planet. Doesn't look like it should have an atmosphere, but sensors show life. Even the moons look promising. In the middle of everything, and yet totally unknown. What a discovery! And it's all mine!"

Landing on the second planet, she notes the jungles and the huge lizardlike creatures that approach her ship. Her transport, a strange silver thing from the sky, has them a little nervous, but she's quite thankful—she might not even be half a mouthful for some of those things! She meets the Tarasin, a native species, and tells them of the galaxy outside their world, grand stories that are met with more than a touch of skepticism. She takes samples of minerals and gases

from various planets and then departs. Reporting to the Republic Bureau of Exploration and Colonization, she names the system Reidi Artom VI. Reidi Artom I through V didn't prove particularly profitable, but she's got a good feeling about VI.

Weeks later, a records search reveals ancient notations made by the Jedi. The system's older name is assigned to the discovery. From that moment on, both the system and its second planet are known as Cularin. Reidi Artom returns to explore further, making herself a hero among the locals. She stays for nearly a quarter of a century. During that time, she charts much of the system and its features.

Months after Reidi's return, the first outsiders arrive, representing a tibanna gas mining company. The company establishes the first floating city in the clouds of Genarius, a planetary gas giant. More outsiders follow, and the harvesting of the system's resources begins. The Tarasin look on with curiosity, but fight back with surprising ferocity when a human company begins to tear the trees from their homeworld. Eventually the outsiders strike a treaty with the Tarasin, and further bloodshed is averted. A friendship develops, strained at first, but it grows as the Tarasin and the outsiders get to know one another and pursue their disparate agendas.

As more and more aliens arrive on Cularin, the Tarasin worry about the future of their home. Fearing further attacks, aliens build cities on huge platforms that rise above the forest canopy, preserving the natural resources and giving the aliens places to call home. In a matter of decades, only a few settlements remain on ground level. These include Gadren and Hedrett—the twin cities originally settled by Reidi Artom and her crew—and some of the oldest Tarasin cities. Spaceports develop on the floating platforms, inexorably linking Cularin to the galaxy at large.

The Coming of the Jedi

Excitement builds around activity in Cularin as rich natural resources are exported. The Jedi return, probing the system with the Force. Sensing a powerful taint of the dark side surrounding the ancient Sith fortress, they send two Jedi consulars to explore.

One of the consulars, Kibh Jeen, is nearly ready to take his trials. His master, Qornah, has trained him well. He is certain that their current mission is a threat they can handle. Since the Jedi Council has reported that the ancient dark side site is dormant, Qornah pilots his shuttle down to the surface with confidence. Always ready to ignore the unpleasant side of existence, he does not feel the pull of evil. Behind him, his Padawan learner, Kibh Jeen, struggles silently.

The shuttle lands. Two Jedi step onto the kaluthin-covered surface and walk toward the half-buried fortress. As Qornah probes with the Force, he does not hear the whispers that press against his apprentice's mind. Kibh Jeen succumbs to whispered temptations, cutting his master down from

REIDI ARTOM, EXPLORER

Reidi Artom, a Near-Human whose species lives for hundreds of years, discovered that she loved excitement, discovery, and the thrill of exploration. She never understood why her people remained on their own planet. So much of the galaxy remained open to them if they only wanted to take it. Sensing opportunity, she escaped from her homeworld at an early age and never looked back. For years, she wandered among the stars, taking life as it came and doing whatever it took to get from one place to another.

Her big break came when a ship she had stowed aboard, a scout vessel, came under attack. The pilot was killed instantly, and the ship was left floating in space. Reidi was able to make repairs to the hyperdrive and get to a starport. After she registered the ship again under her own name, the galaxy opened up before her.

Realizing that the best way to see new worlds was to get paid for it, she became a scout for the Republic and surveyed new systems. While most scouts were sent into the Unknown Regions or the Outer Rim, she went into the Exploration Region to find planets others had missed. Her first discovery, Artom, still bears her name. Later discoveries followed local or ancient names, but she is credited with renewed interest in at least eight systems.

Reidi was last seen about 175 years ago. At that time, she was headed for the Unknown Regions. Whether she is dead or alive

remains to be seen, but the life span of her species is long enough that she may still be exploring.

Reidi Artom: Female Near-Human Fringer 2/Scout 10; Init +2; Defense 21 (+9 class, +2 Dex); Spd 10 m; VP/WP 74/17; Atk +10/+5 ranged (3d6, blaster pistol); SA Adaptive learning (Sense Motive), barter, Skill Mastery (Computer Use, Hide, Search, Pilot), trailblazing, uncanny dodge; SV Fort +10, Ref +9, Will +7; SZ M; FP 3; Rep 3; Str 13, Dex 15, Con 14, Int 14, Wis 15, Cha 13.

Equipment: Three blaster pistols, extra power packs, clothing, environmental suit, flight suit, survival and exploratory gear, scout starship *Trailblazer*.

Skills: Astrogate +15, Climb +7, Computer Use +15, Hide +15, Knowledge (Cularin system) +12, Knowledge (spacer lore) +9, Listen +15, Pilot +19, Repair +17, Search +11, Sense Motive +5, Spot +10, Survival +15; Read/Write Basic, Speak Basic.

Feats: Alertness, Gearhead, Point Blank Shot, Sharp-Eyed, Spacer, Starship Operation (space transport), Toughness, Weapon Group Proficiencies (blaster pistols, blaster rifles, simple weapons).

Note: These statistics describe Reidi at the time she left for Unknown Space.

behind. Stepping over the body, he approaches the walls of the fortress and disappears.

Months later, Kibh Jeen returns. Strong in the dark side, he plans to subjugate the system and lash out at the Jedi Council. Piloting the shuttle into space, he searches for minions who would make useful tools. Pirates in the asteroid belt suit his purposes admirably. In an almost thoughtless display of power, he dominates their minds, and through them, attracts others to his service. An army grows. After his servants sabotage a local power plant, he unleashes his anger at the floating cities of Genarius. Lightning arcs through the great clouds, destroying hundreds of homes as his followers scream through the streets, blasters white-hot. Thousands die.

Kibh Jeen's infamous assault lauches the Dark Jedi Conflict, one of the bloodiest periods in the system's history. Over the next few years, the pirates prove reliably mindless tools. From their base in the asteroid belt, they strike and disappear, hiding their ships in craters, crevasses, and the strange clusters of asteroids that spin together throughout the belt. The system's inhabitants cannot find them, let alone eliminate them. Warships stop all incoming transports. Innocents suffer. Kibh Jeen takes delight in his enemies' failure, but he also feels despair deep in his soul.

Finally, a Jedi Knight and her Padawan come to Cularin to end the crisis. They organize the system's inhabitants and

trading companies. Directed by the Force, their armada finds the pirates and, after a fierce space battle, crushes the pirate fleet. Kibh Jeen does not escape. He is cut down when the Jedi maneuver him into a vulnerable position. Perhaps his own conscience, never truly destroyed by the dark side, plays some small part in his defeat.

After this regrettable incident, the Jedi decide to maintain a permanent presence near the fortress to study it and ward off its evil. The Council begins a school for Jedi training on Almas, on the far side from the fortress. The school prospers, and the continual reminder of evil nearby keeps students dedicated to their studies. The story of Kibh Jeen is told to each new generation of Jedi, in remembrance of what can happen when one is too sure of one's beliefs.

Years pass, and a Twi'lek Jedi Master named Nerra Ziveri assumes the position of Academy Headmaster. Ziveri, already powerful in the Force, turns his attention to probing the dark side aura in earnest. During these years, he trains a promising student named Lanius Qel-Bertuk to take his place. Visions of the future reveal what he must do. Finally, he penetrates the aura of the site and feels the depth of the Sith influence. He calls Lanius and tells him to take charge of the academy. Without explanation, Ziveri disappears from known space and the senses of the Jedi. What happened to him remains a mystery, but Lanius proudly continues Ziveri's tradition of teaching the living Force.

The Tarasin Revolt

Life on Cularin itself is never completely harmonious. The Tarasin live in their jungles, the aliens remain in their cities, and the various cultures do what they can to get along. The Tarasin, sensitive to the Force, believe they should live in harmony with the land, as they have always done, rather than exploiting its bounty as the newcomers do. They try to help the aliens understand. To some extent, they succeed. But even in the Republic, native species sometimes suffer at the expense of progress or the desires of the wealthy. Cularin is no exception.

The first signs of hostility come when the Tarasin bar certain companies from entering the jungle to harvest rare trees. They then declare the ch'hala trees sacred to their religion. Words escalate into violence. Soon the trading companies decide they have to send armed troops down with their workers and droids to avoid losing valuable equipment. Tarasin reprisals are swift and deadly. The Tarasin tribes demonstrate that they've learned to use the technology of their alien opponents, and their natural ability with the Force makes them difficult to stop. The Jedi refuse to intervene.

The Trade Federation, holding major interests on Cularin, sends a force of war droids to secure their operations and protect their crews. The droids interpret their instructions far too loosely, and a number of Tarasin die in a brutal raid. This outrage provokes a series of violent counterattacks. Word spreads among the Tarasin, who prepare to remove all aliens from their world.

With the sanctity of the system at stake, two Jedi consulars come from the academy to negotiate peace. Months of careful discussion follow, but the Tarasin refuse to give in to outsider demands. Meanwhile, minor skirmishes result in the destruction of property and lives. After six months of negotiations, diplomats establish an accord called the Cularin Compact. In this agreement, they articulate the rights of the Tarasin and sharply curtail the outsiders' ability to harm the planet. Peace comes slowly after that, but the Tarasin and aliens work together to harvest the resources of the planet while protecting its delicate ecological balance.

Rise in Crime

Where legitimate trade flourishes, illicit trade follows. As Cularin's prosperity grows, incidents of piracy become more frequent. Shipments disappear, and smugglers bring in illegal goods. For some time the criminals act independently, but crime attracts the interest of an exiled Hutt named Riboga. Bringing the famed Hutt talent for organization with him, he gathers the criminals into a small syndicate. The pirates form their own gang. Conflict between the two groups escalates as the years pass.

The costs of running operations in Cularin also rise year by year. Unstable gravity wells make space travel to the system expensive. The costs associated with losses to the pirates

make Riboga rethink his desire to do business there. As a result, he is not at all angry to lose the whole operation to his assistant, a strange alien named Nirama, in a sabacc game. When the last hand is revealed, Riboga laughs a throaty Hutt laugh and returns to Nal Hutta without looking back. What Riboga does not know is that Nirama has been skimming profits, faking accounts to make his operations look unprofitable. Through this strategy, he gains control of the criminal empire without incurring the Hutt's wrath or having to kill him, an act that surely would have brought its own hideous consequences.

Trade Wars

The Cularin Compact brings protection to the planet and the Tarasin, but the Trade Federation sees it as an opportunity. Any contract has loopholes, and they are determined to exploit this one as they do every other. By manipulating terms, using dirty tricks, and employing a little outright sabotage, the Trade Federation drives its competitors out of the system. It seizes control of all legal trade in Cularin and holds it. The smugglers and Riboga the Hutt maintain control of illegal trade.

Decades later, trouble rears its head again in the Trade Federation. The Neimoidians, the leaders of the Trade Federation, make a deal to blockade a small planet in another system. Fearing the consequences of failure, two of the other races, the Filordi and the Caarites, break with the Neimoidians and form their own trade organization, the Metatheran Cartel.

While the Neimoidians pay attention to a powerful new client, the Filordi and Caarites scheme on a different front. They deduce that the Trade Federation can be dislodged from Cularin, and they are correct. The Metatheran Cartel begins by exposing the policies the Trade Federation has used to drive out competition and keep labor costs low. They begin direct competition with the Federation in its major market areas and invite other races, including the Sullustans, to start operations within the system.

But the Trade Federation is not completely ignorant of the Cularin situation. The Neimoidians realize they need income and resources from the system if they are to recover any kind of position as a trade leader. Lacking the resources to make direct confrontations, they hire pirates from the asteroid belt to harass Metatheran shipping and facilities. These attacks grow more desperate as the Neimoidians suffer heavily in another part of the galaxy: the Naboo system.

The conflict between the two trading groups would last for months, or even years, if not for two circumstances. First, some of the species allied with the Metatheran Cartel express their displeasure with the strategies both sides are using, complaining of dropping business and rising prices. The Cartel also notices the costs of the conflict and decides to attempt to buy out the pirates. At first unwilling to listen, the pirates begin considering the counteroffer. The

Neimoidians have not paid them for their work, after all, and the Cartel has credits to spend in the system. Furthermore, the Cartel has made significant progress in ousting the Trade Federation from its primary markets in the system.

The decision becomes critical when a group of Naboo natives defeats the Neimoidians. Word spreads that the Neimoidians might lose their trade charter. Such a loss would mean that the pirates would not get paid—so they immediately switch sides. The Trade Federation's activities in the system collapse, and it withdraws.

The Cartel, in light of this victory, lessens its own trade activities, trying to gauge the demand of Cularin's inhabitants and establish better business practices. It also takes a few tips from the Trade Federation and begins using some of the very practices it decried during the trade struggle.

Cularin Today

It is a year since the defeat of the Trade Federation at Naboo. The Metatheran Cartel has tightened its grip on trade and turned on the pirates it allied with in trade conflicts. Patrol craft are hunting pirate vessels in the asteroid belts, but failing to stop piracy. Smugglers thrive under the new restrictions that the Cartel has put on trade. Independent companies, invited into the system by the Cartel, have refused to be dislodged. The SoroSuub Corporation has built a floating manufacturing city in the clouds of Genarius, supplying speeders and starships. Gambling havens thrive deeper in the clouds of Genarius, as do other unsavory elements.

Investors have completed terraforming of Almas's moon, Dorumaa. They've opened a resort center that draws wealthy guests from insystem and beyond. Nirama continues to run a profitable criminal empire, despite problems with pirates. Tarasin continue their simple lifestyle and ensure that aliens are abiding by the Cularin Compact. Many Padawan learners in the Almas Academy have become Jedi Knights and taken students of their own. Others have stayed at the school to teach, or left the system to follow the will of the Force. The academy continues its vigil over the ancient fortress, and notes with concern the slowly spreading deadness on the far side of Almas.

Cularin has become a member of the Republic. A senator elected on Cularin has taken her place in the Senate on Coruscant. Official recognition has attracted official interest, and Republic military vessels have arrived in the system. Under the command of Colonel Jir Tramsig, the Republic has established a military base on Cularin and a second base on Dorumaa. Unknown to the inhabitants of the system, there is a third secret base on one of Genarius's moons, Ostfrei.

Rumors circulate that another Dark Jedi has come to Cularin, but no one can produce proof of his or her existence. The rumors do not lie, however. Master Lanius Qel-Bertuk has begun searching the system for this new threat that only he can feel.

Cularin System Catalog

Though the Cularian system has easy access to the Corellian Spine Trade Route, one of the main trade routes in the known galaxy, it has only recently attracted attention from the galaxy at large. The reason for this apparent isolation lies in the strange gravitic anomalies found there. First, the cores of three of the planets are extremely dense, resulting in larger hyperspace gravity reflections than the bodies would normally generate. The larger gravity wells overlap periodically in hyperspace, making the disturbance even worse. Jumps into the Cularin system under these conditions are extremely difficult for normal nav computer programs, but they can be done.

Gravity reflections within the system are not the only problem. The whole system is surrounded by a dense cloud of comets, remnants from the system's formation. Most have dense cores similar to the heavier planets in the system, and as they pursue their erratic courses, they interact with each other. Occasionally they collide, showering frozen debris and creating smaller comets that take their place in the strange cosmic dance.

Because of these two dangers, the safest way to travel to the system is to arrive at a point just outside the comet cloud, read the current behavior of the comets, and then make the calculations for a second jump into the system itself. Larger ships arrive at the outside edge of the asteroid belt and proceed with sublight engines to their final destinations.

Some daring pilots attempt to approach the system from above its plane, but this route is only a little more successful than the traditional approach. The comets still pose a problem. Because of their constant deflections off each other, the comet cloud extends in a nearly spherical pattern around the system. Thus, even when using a course that bypasses the asteroid belt, pilots must stop to analyze the comet distribution before dealing with the larger hyperspace gravity shadows.

After arriving, a visitor is first drawn to the two suns in mutual orbit. Morasil was the first star to form. The ancient yellow sun is perhaps as old as the galaxy itself, and it has shrunk in its long lifetime. Alone, it produces a cold, dim light that cannot reach the asteroid belt. Its partner, Termadus, is a white dwarf star. Much younger than Morasil, it has nonetheless sped through its solar lifetime. Now it draws gases from the corona of Morasil, creating a gaseous haze between the two stars. Together, they give the luminous equivalent of a single bright star, creating a gravitational hyperspace shadow much larger than the realspace area taken by their orbits.

Acilaris

The closest planet to the twin suns, Acilaris could be mistaken for a large asteroid, but definitely warrants planetary status. Acilaris has enough gravity to hold an atmos-

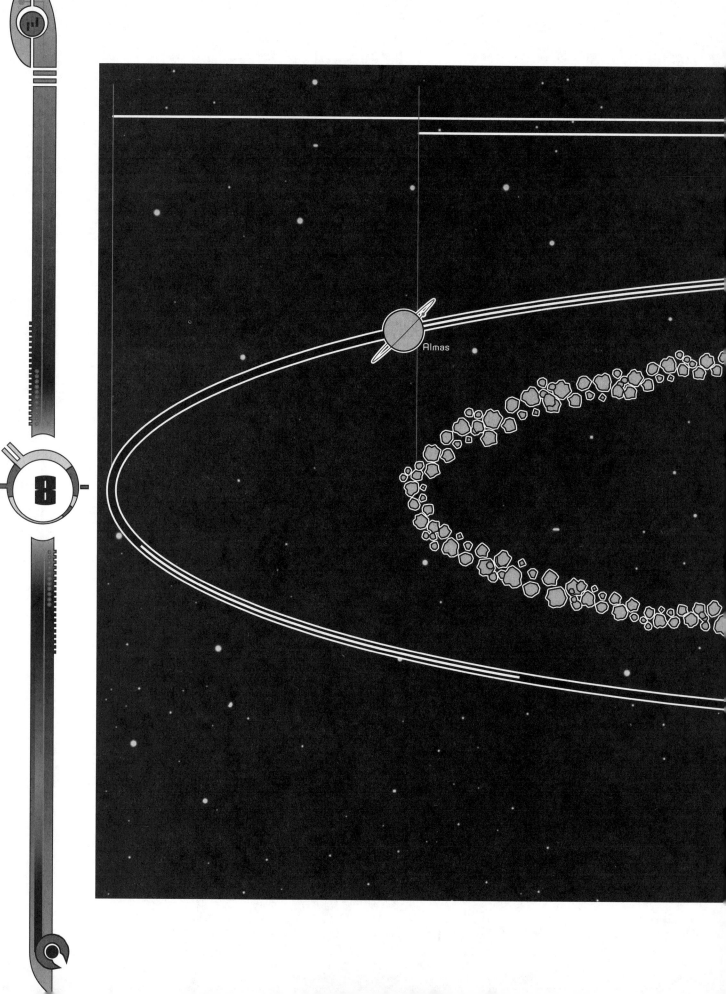

Almas

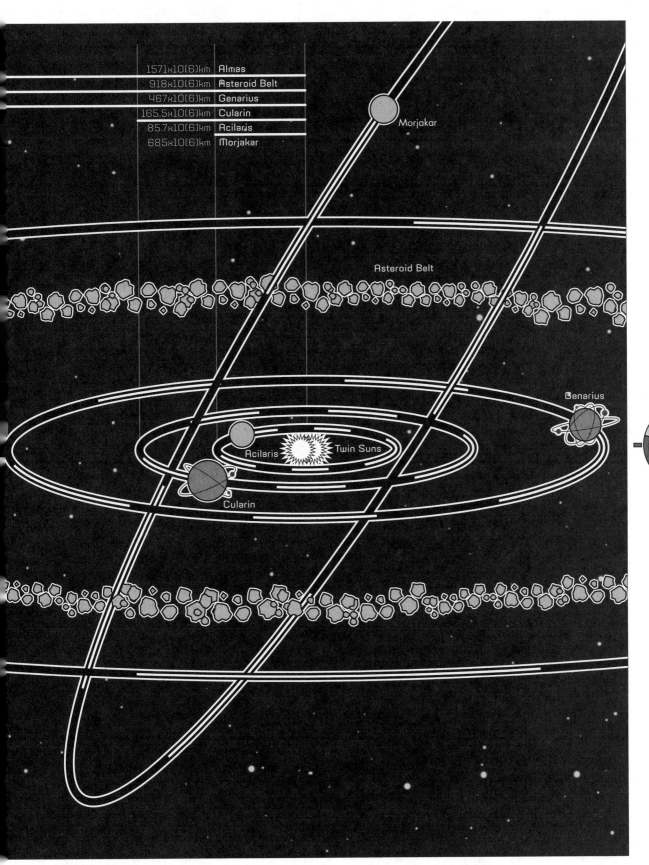

1571×10(6)km	Almas
918×10(6)km	Asteroid Belt
467×10(6)km	Genarius
165.5×10(6)km	Cularin
85.7×10(6)km	Acilaris
685×10(6)km	Morjakar

Morjakar

Asteroid Belt

Genarius

Acilaris

Twin Suns

Cularin

Asteroid Belt

> **Acilaris at a Glance**
> **Type:** Barren rock
> **Climate:** None
> **Length of Day:** 9 standard hours
> **Length of Year:** 112 standard days

phere composed of light gases. Survival gear is definitely required.

Because of its proximity to the suns, Acilaris has a very hot surface temperature. The surface is far too hot for ships to land safely. Thus, no one has been able to visit it. Sensor scans of its emissions show a variety of rare minerals and even some crystals. The presence of these minerals in other planets of the system has kept the various mining consortiums from attempting expeditions to Acilaris. However, unconfirmed reports say that at least one company has contracted with the droids of Uffel to produce special machinery that could withstand the conditions and begin mining.

Cularin

> **Cularin at a Glance**
> **Type:** Terrestrial
> **Climate:** Jungle, mountainous jungle
> **Length of Day:** 22 standard hours
> **Length of Year:** 300 standard days

Cularin, the system's namesake planet, is covered in lush rain forests and jungles. Mountain ranges reach through the trees and almost touch the skies, forming plains and deep valleys between them. Thick trees cover the whole planet, except in a few places where logging companies have been active in years past. The climate is mild and humid, reaching uncomfortably high temperatures during the height of summer. At night, the inhabitants enjoy cool temperatures. Rain falls almost every day, though not strongly enough to disrupt activities or threaten lives.

Among the planet's many trees are a number of rare hardwoods and the mysterious ch'hala trees. Ch'hala trees are tall with thick drooping foliage. Their greenish-purple bark produces swirling color patterns across the planet's surface. The Tarasin natives claim the trees are not native to the world. Some of the softer woods are highly prized, attracting great interest from various corporations.

Cularin is a world rich in lifeforms. Great lizards called kilassin occupy the top of the food chain. Of the many varieties of kilassin that live deep in the jungles, most are omnivorous, but some prefer live prey to plants. As settlements continue to appear, the lumbering beasts are driven farther from civilization. A few have been captured and domesticated. Corporations such as the Metatheran Cartel use them as labor beasts when they cannot take repulsorsleds into the jungles.

Much farther down the food chain, small creatures called mulissiki scavenge for food. Commonly seen around Tarasin settlements, these scavengers keep villages clean by devouring waste just about as fast as it is produced. Because they scurry away from any approaching creature, they do not really pose a problem to the Tarasin. In the cities, however, mulissiki are a nuisance. Once they get into the platform cities, they cannot escape. Instead, they make nests in whatever dark corners they can find.

The mountain ranges that cut through Cularin's jungles reach beyond the clouds. The lower ridges support Tarasin villages and other life, but the higher reaches are devoid of all creatures except mulissiki. One range, the Kiallquis, has a sheer face that is particularly suited to speeder racing and mountain climbing. In the past, the Tarasin used it to test the truth claims of suspected criminals (by lowering them over the edge), but in modern times, the ridge is used more for sponsored speeder races.

Natives

The intelligent natives of Cularin are called Tarasin. These sentients are remotely related to the great kilassin. Both evolved from the same ancestors, but along different paths. Tarasin developed a tribal society, while the kilassin continued to migrate in herds. Tarasin tribes, called irstats, usually contain between thirty and fifty members. Larger tribes also exist. For instance, the Hiironi irstat contains more than three hundred members. However, most Tarasin prefer smaller tribes and simpler lives.

The Tarasin believe they maintain a symbiotic relationship with their world, a belief that motivates their religion. Through an attunement to the natural world, Tarasin can sense the Force naturally. Traditionally, their religious figures have become Force adepts, but their race did not fully understand the Force until Jedi came to the system. Their religion is based around a simple appreciation for nature. They sense life around them through their quills and value it too much to break the circle of symbiosis. Because of this spiritual closeness, Tarasin do not travel very far from Cularin for extended periods. In fact, they are fiercely protective of their world and its resources, violently protecting it from outsiders. This attitude has forced them into conflict with offworlders twice in their history.

Originally, Tarasin were too quick to trust offworlders. Visitors found the exotic woods of the forests impressive, and the Tarasin sensed their interest. As a friendly gesture, they began harvesting these commodities immediately. Tarasin methods were slow compared to the demand of the galaxy at large. When offworlders began tearing down the forests themselves, conflicts resulted. Since then, the Tarasin have learned to compromise. The best example of this is the Cularin Compact, an agreement protecting the kilassin, the minerals of the planet, and most importantly, the forests. In Tarasin religion, the most unique trees on the planet, the ch'hala, are sacred. As part of their compromise, Tarasin now

Tarasin

The Tarasin are a tribal species of reptilian humanoids with a rich oral tradition. Most tribes are small (only a few dozen Tarasin each) and led by a chieftain, usually the second oldest female in the tribe. They refer to the eldest female in the tribe simply as "Mother," holding her up as a model of perfection.

Personality: Calm, communal, curious, fiercely protective of their world and its resources. Tarasin rarely get violently angry unless their world or their tribes are threatened.

Physical Description: Reptilian humanoids. The average Tarasin stands about 1.6 to 1.7 meters tall. Its body is covered in translucent scales. The skin beneath the scales changes color. When one is frightened or angry, a multicolored "fan" of thin, scaly flesh spreads out around a Tarasin's head.

Tarasin Homeworld: Most of Cularin is a tropical rain forest.

Language: Tarasin speak their own language, Tarasinese. Their hunters also use a silent form of communication that relies on their color-changing skin.

Names: Dariana, Sa'Alana, Ta'Sen.

Adventurers: Most Tarasin adventurers are curious about offworlders and new traditions. Fringers and scouts are very common. A growing number of Tarasin take up the traditions of the Jedi. Force-users prefer the Force adept class and often serve as religious leaders.

Tarasin Species Traits

- +2 Intelligence, –2 Strength.
- Medium-size.
- Tarasin base speed is 10 meters.
- +4 species bonus to Fortitude saves against heat hazards.
- +4 species bonus to Hide checks.
- +2 species bonus to See Force checks (only Tarasin Force-users with the requisite feats gain this bonus).
- Silent Communication. The Tarasin's color-changing scales allow it to communicate silently with any other Tarasin within 10 meters. Members of other species who learn to interpret this language (by spending the requisite skill points) may understand it, but can never "speak" it.
- –2 penalty to Bluff and Sense Motive checks. The Tarasin's color-changing scales, as well as the multicolored fan, make hiding emotions difficult. Because of this, they also have difficulty detecting deceit.

Kilassin

Kilassin, though native to Cularin, resemble great lizards and dinosaurs from other planets in the galaxy. Kilassin come in many colors, ranging from the subtle to the glaringly obvious. Color does not seem to hinder their hunting ability. Some offworlders have reported seeing the same kilassin as one color one day and a different color the next. Tarasin reply that the offworlder must have seen two similar kilassin.

Kilassin come in two main body types with individual variations. Some are long and thin with long legs; they rise up to survey their domains as towering, bipedal stalkers. Others are more compact and dense, shambling through the jungle as gargantuan, lumbering behemoths. All kilassin can walk on four legs, though most can walk on hind legs for brief periods and attack with their forelegs. Kilassin claws are thick and long, capable of digging into dead tree trunks for worms or ripping the throats from smaller creatures. Most have mouths full of teeth, but the teeth are adapted to varying foods and designed more for grinding than tearing.

Kilassin do not handle heat well. During the hottest parts of the year, they retreat to large lakes or deep forested valleys, where they survive by eating fleshy plants and (occasionally) each other. During the cool parts of the year, they roam the planet in a nomadic fashion, staying in place only long enough to breed young, grab a meal, or sleep. Kilassin sometimes bring down prey that's too large to eat in one sitting. When this happens, they leave the half-eaten carcass behind for other kilassin to find.

Kilassin attack with their claws, not their jaws. They bring down prey and rip it apart with their claws before eating. Claws take the place of sharp flesh-ripping teeth, so that they can also chew and digest plant matter. Kilassin do not generally attack creatures except when hungry. They flee from needless conflict, and modern weapons scare them off immediately.

Kilassin: Herd Animal or Predator 5; Init +0; Defense 14 (–2 size, +6 natural); Spd 20 m; VP/WP 52/36; Atk +8/+8 melee (1d6+7, claws); SQ Low-light vision, +4 species bonus on Swim checks; SV Fort +8, Ref +3, Will +1; SZ H; Rep 0; Str 22, Dex 10, Con 18, Int 2, Wis 10, Cha 9.

Skills: Listen +4, Spot +4, Survival +2.

Feats: Cleave, Power Attack, Track.

Mulissiki

A mulissik is a meter-long, four-legged creature with smooth skin, a long, thin tail, and a long nose. Its skin is primarily brown with irregular streaks of green and white. A mulissik can bend its prehensile nose to search in trees and mounds for refuse. It usually lives off the waste of other creatures. Although it's not very particular about what kind of waste it devours, it is also a finicky creature that likes to keep clean. After rooting through a mound of smelly refuse, it makes for the nearest waterhole or river to clean itself off. It really enjoys the bathing process, almost as much as it enjoys getting dirty. Whiskerlike antennae on its face help it sense its surroundings. Mulissiki are completely deaf, relying on their whiskers to feel pressure changes in the air.

Mulissiki congregate around sources of refuse, but can be found almost everywhere on Cularin, even on the highest mountain ranges. The creatures thrive even when there is no apparent food. They can be quite tasty themselves, but must be cooked thoroughly for Human or Tarasin consumption. The huge kilassin only hunt mulissiki that are clean or in the process of cleaning.

Mulissiki do not attack large creatures. They can, but they don't; instead, they cower and hide. When really threatened, they emit a stinky cloud of gas that requires anyone within 20 meters of the creature to make a Will save (DC 12) or flee.

Mulissik: Scavenger 1; Init +4; Defense 17 (+1 size, +4 Dex, +2 natural); Spd 25 m; VP/WP 6/14; Atk +4 melee (1d4-2, bite); SQ Low-light vision, stink gas cloud (Will save DC 12); SV Fort +3, Ref +6, Will +0; SZ S; Rep 0; Str 7, Dex 19, Con 14, Int 3, Wis 10, Cha 7.

Skills: Hide +6, Spot +4, Survival +2.

Feats: Weapon Finesse (bite).

allow offworlders to claim a few of these trees each year. Each must be transplanted and taken offworld alive.

Tarasin are ominivorous, but usually prefer plants native to Cularin. Their species used to avoid eating meat, but as they moved closer to Human cities, they adjusted their diet. Tarasin still do not eat animals except in the company of offworlders. Although they hunt kilassin for their skins, bones, and organs (which are medicinal, according to the tribal elders), they find the idea of hunting them for food very distasteful.

Tarasin villages contain small buildings; each one shelters one or two sentients. Residences were once made of wood and plants, but are now built from modules of prefab materials imported from offworld. Structures are often integrated with the surrounding tree branches. The buildings, even prefab ones, fit so well into the surrounding trees that it is sometimes possible to walk right through a Tarasin village without realizing it.

Most villages look extremely temporary. Many first-time visitors think an entire village could easily be packed up and moved the next day. This is not true. Tarasin irstats very rarely live a nomadic lifestyle. The villages contain common buildings for craft and industry, living spaces, and storage buildings. After their oldest settlements were devastated by Trade Federation war droids, Tarasin have learned to use modern tools and weapons. In a local village, it is as

common to see stored blaster power packs as it is to see kilassin skins or food.

Tarasin tribes elect the second eldest female as chief. She assumes the title of Irstat-Kes, which means "tribal leader." Their society is not matriarchal in the sense that females dominate. In Tarasin culture, females remain in the villages while male Tarasin hunt for resources. Thus, it makes sense that someone who is at the village should be the leader. The oldest female of each irstat becomes a wise woman whom the Tarasin call "Mother." Tarasin Mothers embody the best aspects of the Tarasin way of life, and all look up to them. Tarasin Irstat-Kes and Mothers are often Force adepts as well, although this is not required.

The largest tribe, the Hiironi, has settled near the only offworld towns on the surface of the planet. Reidi Artom opened her negotiations with the Irstat-Kes of the Hiironi, not realizing that one tribe is no more important than another among the Tarasin. The Hiironi irstat was smaller hundreds of years ago. Twelve tribes lived near Cloud Mountain, the highest peak on the planet. Tarasin used to say that the top of the peak was made of clouds, not rock—hence the name. Cloud Mountain proved them wrong when it erupted, causing an earthquake in the mountain range. Rock and lava rained down on the jungle for days. When the rocks stopped falling, the tribes came out of hiding and joined together for mutual aid (in the Tarasin language,

"Hiironi" means "different but together"). The irstat stayed together and moved farther from the mountain. Now the mountain serves as a focal point for many other tribes, largely because of its size.

Dariana, Mother of the Hiironi

The most ancient and wise of all the Tarasin, Dariana is no longer the paragon everyone believes her to be. She is indeed wise, but she is also selfish, working for her own good as much as the good of all Tarasin or the Hiironi itstat. Dariana was never Irstat-Kes. Her sister Meirana was slightly older than she was and more capable; thus, Meirana assumed leadership. Dariana was at first content, but later wanted more of a role in the tribe's affairs. When the previous Mother was accidentally killed by a kilassin, Meiriana was chosen as Mother and Dariana was selected to be the new Irstat-Kes. This arrangement was just what Dariana wanted, but within a day, a strange disease killed Meirana. Other Force adepts said that she was called to be one with the world. Dariana found herself as Mother instead of the leadership role she wanted. She truly tries to fulfill her role, but she chafes when her wisdom is not heeded.

Wizened yet still tall, Dariana wears the traditional robe of the Mother well. She carries a blaster pistol because, as she told the children one evening, wisdom may be the most powerful force in the life of the Tarasin, but it is not more powerful than a running kilassin. Her eyes, gray with age, look upon the world with a little disillusionment. Her skin no longer changes colors, and she rarely leaves the village of the Hiironi, but she still manages to be present at any important talks between Tarasin and offworlders. She is nearing the end of her life. The closer she comes to death, the more involved she wants to be in life.

Dariana: Female Tarasin Force Adept 16; Init –1; Defense 18 (–1 Dex, +9 class); Spd 10 m; VP/WP 52/11; Atk +11/+6/+1 melee (1d6, quarterstaff; see below); +11/+6/+1 ranged (3d6, blaster pistol); SA Comprehend speech, Force talisman, and Force Quarterstaff (see below); SQ +4 species bonus to Survival checks in heat conditions, –2 species penalty to Bluff and Sense Motive checks; SV Fort +9, Ref +6, Will +13; SZ M; FP 7; Rep 18; DSP 2; Str 9, Dex 9, Con 11, Int 16, Wis 17, Cha 10.

   Equipment: Force Quarterstaff (use 3 vitality to get +2d4 damage bonus for 16 rounds); Force Talisman (+4 Force bonus to saving throws against Force skills and Force feats).

   Skills: Craft (cooking) +13, Craft (weaponsmithing) +11, Handle Animal +4, Hide +5, Knowledge (Cularin–flora and fauna) +19, Listen +15, Sense Motive +13, Spot +13, Survival +15, Swim +9, Treat Injury +11; Speak Basic, Speak Tarasinese, Understand silent Tarasin color language.

   Force Skills: Affect Mind +6, Empathy +17, Enhance Senses +11, Farseeing +12, Force Grip +9, Move Object +7, See Force +19.

   Feats: Dodge, Fame, Great Fortitude, Quickness,

Trustworthy, Weapon Group Proficiencies (blaster pistols, primitive weapons, simple weapons).

   Force Feats: Alter, Control, Dissipate Energy, Force-Sensitive, Sense.

Cryalira, Irstat-Kes of the Hiironi

Cryalira is surprised to find herself as Irstat-Kes. She expected that she might gain the title someday in the distant future, but Meirana's sudden death immediately thrust her into the spotlight. A skilled hunter, Cryalira would rather be roaming the jungle than presiding over the Hiironi or interacting with the Humans in Gadrin. She believes that she is not trained for her current position, and that she does not have the natural talent to succeed. Her reluctance shows in her decisions, or lack of decisions, frequently.

For a Tarasin, she is pretty. Her scales are very neat, her eyes are a clear blue, and her skin fan is very attractive. She tends to use it when she is presiding, confusing everyone by making them think she is angry. Thus, by accident, she overcomes her own nervousness. She is growing into her position. Given a little more time, she could be an excellent Irstat-Kes. Whether she will have the time, only the Force knows, as one or two malcontents in her tribe plot against her leadership.

Cryalira: Female Tarasin Scout 12; Init +2; Defense 20 (+8 class, +2 Dex); Spd 10 m; VP/WP 84/15; Atk +12/+7 melee (1d8+3, spear), +11/+6 ranged (3d6, blaster pistol); SA Skill Mastery (Hide, Search, Listen, Survival), trailblazing, uncanny dodge; SQ +4 species bonus to Survival checks in heat conditions, –2 species penalty to Bluff and Sense Motive checks; SV Fort +8, Ref +8, Will +7; SZ M; FP 6; Rep 11; Str 16, Dex 14, Con 15, Int 15, Wis 13, Cha 14.

   Skills: Climb +12, Diplomacy +6, Hide +17, Listen +15, Knowledge (Cularin–flora and fauna) +14, Move Silently +12, Search +10, Spot +15, Survival +19, Swim +7, Treat Injury +7; Speak Tarasinese, Understand Tarasin silent color language.

   Force Skills: See Force +6.

   Feats: Alertness, Dodge, Mobility, Skill Emphasis (Survival), Track, Weapon Group Proficiencies (blaster pistols, blaster rifles, simple weapons).

   Force Feats: Force-Sensitive, Sense.

Fisonna

Fissona is a nine-year-old Tarasin child. He's a troublemaker in the Hiironi irstat. His parents don't manage him well, and his natural liveliness often gets him into trouble. He is the grandson of Cryalira, the Irstat-Kes, but his position doesn't prevent him from being caught and punished. When encountered, he is either running from trouble or sitting with his young friends thinking up a grand scheme against Humans in the nearby towns. His redeeming virtue is that he knows everything that happens in the Hiironi village. Unfortunately, this is because he listens at doors and spies on his tribemates.

As young Tarasin go, he looks average, but he has developed good control with his color-changing ability. He wears medallions he carves from rocks and branches. They do not show any talent on his part, but he likes his own work and has a higher opinion of himself than is warranted.

Fissona: Male Tarasin Fringer 1; Init +2; Defense 15 (+3 class, +2 Dex); Spd 10 m; VP/WP 8/11; Atk +0 melee, +0 ranged; SQ +4 species bonus to Survival checks in heat conditions, –2 species penalty to Bluff and Sense Motive checks; SV Fort +2, Ref +3, Will +2; SZ M; FP 0; Rep 0; Str 12, Dex 15, Con 11, Int 13, Wis 15, Cha 12.

Skills: Climb +2, Hide +6, Listen +3, Spot +4, Survival +3; Speak Tarasinese, Understand Tarasin silent color language.

Feats: Alertness, Quickness, Weapon Group Proficiencies (blaster pistols, simple weapons).

Gadrin and Hedrett

When Reidi Artom first landed on Cularin, she set her ship down in a clearing next to the Estauril, a river almost two kilometers wide. There she met the Hiironi irstat. When she returned, she helped build the original buildings of the first town, Gadrin, where the river flowed into the base of Cloud Mountain. The population expanded quickly, and a second town called Hedrett was started on the other side of the river. Reidi linked the two towns with a great bridge. Soon they became cities and expanded into the jungle. The

Tarasin, seeing unchecked expansion of the cities as bad for their world, opposed any new building. After the Tarasin Revolt, Humans and aliens erected the first platform cities. As more offworlders moved there, Gadrin and Hedrett dwindled into backwater towns.

Gadrin was originally planned on a grid, but rapid expansion during the town's early years caused the leaders to abandon that plan, letting people build wherever they wanted. The buildings are made mostly of wood from the surrounding jungle, but after prefab buildings were brought in, the city became a mixture of wood, metal, and plastic structures. Hedrett held to the grid system much better, and builders in Hedrett used mostly prefab metal construction. Gadrin looks more native and older than its sister town.

In size and population, the two towns are very similar. Gadrin boasts a population of 18,000 offworlders and 2,000 Tarasin. Hedrett rates its population at 16,700 offworlders and 2,900 Tarasin. The similarities end there. The towns have developed as if each was trying to be different from the other, as though the river somehow made the town on the other side a rival or enemy.

A governor rules Gadrin. In theory, the people can elect a new governor every four years. In practice, real elections have not been held in over thirty standard years, and no one really minds. Democracy, the people have found, can be a lot of work. The residents would rather spend their effort on commerce instead. Reidi Artom dreamed that the leaders would serve one term each and then return to private business, so that the duty of government would fall on everyone. Again, practice differs greatly from this ideal. Within the last thirty years, "professional" politicians have changed the electoral system to the extent that the governor appoints other needed officers, and the people ratify his choices with a public vote. No campaigning accompanies these votes. Many of the citizens don't know when elections are held, and they simply don't care. This ignorance results more from apathy than any real attempt to conceal the vote from the citizens. Voting in Gadrin is a formality. If the governor had to choose from a longer list of candidates, he would probably be unable to decide.

Hedrett, on the other hand, governs itself through a Town Council composed of nine senior counselors and twelve junior counselors. Each junior counselor's vote on any matter counts as half that of a senior counselor, so the total number of votes on any issue can be as high as fifteen. Unlike Gadrin, the people on this side of the Estauril participate in their government. They enjoy elections, or at least find them entertaining. Votes on major issues not only attract all the counselors, but a number of citizens who don't have any pressing business at the time. The citizens harangue the counselors and argue with them as if they could also vote, thus prolonging debates. No one can say that the public is not involved in every decision.

Election of counselors follows a similar practice. Elections for empty seats are held with a week's notice. Interested candidates can campaign all they want after they've filed a petition to run for office and made a lengthy speech to the Town Council. Unfortunately for the residents of Hedrett, no major issues of interest have surfaced in two years, not since Senior Counselor Westa Impeveri upset popular favorite Karid Blakken. Blakken had the votes recounted, because he suspected Impeveri of rigging the ballot box, but Impeveri was proven innocent.

Gadrin is closely connected to the platform city of Lissken. It imports as much galactic culture as it can from that spaceport. Holotheatres, opera, concerts, and dance recitals are all available. Of course, most of the people don't attend these displays of culture. The governor enjoys them immensely and has little difficulty spending public credits on what some would call his own entertainment.

Hedrett has its own spaceport, which it uses to premiere music and arts before Gadrin can get them. The original spaceport for Gadrin was built across the river, where there was no city. Hedrett grew up around the spaceport, eventually annexing it officially from Gadrin. Gadrin's governor, Barnab Chistor, has since authorized the building of a second spaceport, but plans have not even been completed. Hedrett's docking bays are so convenient that no one really sees a need for another facility closer to Gadrin.

Gadrin is the home of a unique cultural feature. Because this was Reidi Artom's first settlement in the system, Gadrin keeps a memorial to her memory and a museum of her artifacts. Reidi Artom's discoveries throughout the system

brought fame, interest, and credits. She used all three to develop Cularin and advance the level of technology to a standard comparable with the Core Worlds. For this, she is beloved among the residents of both Gadrin and Hedrett. She was also admired among the residents of the platform cities. A statue of Artom fully 20 meters tall graces the front of the museum that holds her logbooks, personal effects, holovids of her travels before reaching Cularin, and other curiosities. The museum is open to all.

With the advent of the platform cities, Gadrin and Hedrett have faded in significance in the affairs of Cularin. The Hiironi irstat lives nearby, but the most advanced commerce takes place in the platform cities. Whether the sister towns can regain some of their former glory, or even want to, remains to be seen.

Barnab Chistor, Governor of Gadrin

Chistor yearned to be an explorer when he was a child, but opportunities never opened up for him. He applied to the university on his homeworld of Alderaan, but was denied admittance. He settled for a lesser school and pursued politics as a second course of study. As he excelled at political courses and failed at technical and scientific ones, he gave up his dream and entered public service. Then he heard about Cularin. There, he reasoned, he would have an opportunity to practice politics and still be an explorer of sorts. The system had just opened up within the last 180 years. The Republic Bureau of Exploration and Colonization would not have found everything yet.

He moved to Gadrin and put his political skills to work. He also convinced a scout ship to take him along on an expedition to Uffel, where he discovered something he had not expected: Exploring is uncomfortable. He could not breathe, he could barely see, and he was in a cramped ship with people who expected him to know more than he did. He did not attempt the life of an explorer again. Instead, he maneuvered himself into the governor's position.

Since becoming governor, he has put on weight, but tries to stay in shape. His blue eyes have been called "piercing," but he does not work to achieve a threatening appearance. He wears his hair short because of the humidity, but always dresses well.

His understanding is only moderate outside the political arena, but as governor, he has really done his best for the residents. He likes his job and does not want to give it up. To preserve it, he works to keep the people as uninterested in politics as possible.

Barnab Chistor: Male Human Diplomat 12; Init +0; Defense 14 (+4 class); Spd 10 m; WP 14; Atk +6/+1 ranged (3d6, blaster pistol); SV Fort +4, Ref +4, Will +9; SZ M; Rep 9; Str 10, Dex 11, Con 11, Int 14, Wis 13, Cha 15.

Skills: Appraise +7, Bluff +12, Computer Use +6, Diplomacy +14, Gather Information +15, Knowledge (alien species—Tarasin) +11, Knowledge (bureaucracy) +10, Knowledge (Cularin system) +12, Knowledge (scholar—

governmental theories) +8, Listen +7, Profession (politician) +12, Sense Motive +9, Spot +6; Read/Write Basic, Speak Basic, Speak Tarasinese.

Feats: Fame, Persuasive, Sharp-Eyed, Skill Emphasis (Gather Information), Toughness, Weapon Group Proficiencies (blaster pistols, simple weapons).

Westa Impeveri, Senior Counselor of Hedrett

Impeveri, like Chistor, is a recent arrival to the Cularin system. Growing up in the Outer Rim, Westa Impeveri served as a spokesman and intermediary in the organizations of several crimelords, all small-time operators. As a result, he was consistently treated very badly. He would pass from one crimelord's service to another because of sabacc game losses, shifting power hierarchies, and frequent assassinations. Eventually, when he grew tired and desperate, he stole away one night in a freighter bound for Corellia. He never made it far. He was discovered and dropped in Hedrett by the crew on its way through.

He would have preferred more advance publicity, but he made the best of his situation, learning everything he could about the town's counselors. He managed to get elected to a junior counselorship, and from that position, he learned a lot of interesting secrets. Westa also hired a great many people to quietly spread the word about him, so that he had soon acquired exactly the reputation and renown he wanted among the residents. Two years ago, he used those secrets to his advantage and ousted a popular senior counselor in his bid for power.

Average in appearance, Impeveri conveys an image of friendly trust and a willingness to be approached. People find themselves confiding in him. Their confidences are filed away with everything else he has learned. As a senior counselor, he has shown competence, but not brilliance, and his apparently open attitude assures him of friends among the other counselors. Impeveri is waiting for the right moment and the right opportunity.

Westa Impeveri: Male Human Diplomat 9; Init +0; Defense 13 (+3 class); Spd 10 m; WP 9; Atk +4 ranged (3d6, blaster pistol); SV Fort +3, Ref +3, Will +7; SZ M; Rep 8; Str 14, Dex 10, Con 11, Int 13, Wis 12, Cha 17.

Skills: Bluff +15, Diplomacy +12, Gather Information +15, Knowledge (politics—Cularin) +9, Knowledge (streetwise—Cularin) +8, Listen +9, Profession (politician) +7, Sense Motive +10; Read/Write Basic, Speak Basic, Speak Tarasinese.

Feats: Fame, Persuasive, Skill Emphasis (Listen), Weapon Group Proficiencies (blaster pistols, simple weapons)

Kim Klib

Kim Klib is a young wastrel employed by one of the emporiums in Gadrin. He works as a messenger and stockboy. His employer is kind to him, but his employer's wife treats him like dirt. He is average in height, thin, blond, and brown-eyed. He wears patched jumpsuits and tries to be unobtrusive at the emporium.

On the side, he works for an underworld mechanic and steals parts from the emporium. He likes stealing and thinks he has a talent for it. He has been lucky so far, but his over-confidence is likely to get him caught. Kim Klib is learning where to make underworld contacts in Gadrin and Hedrett. For a price, he could help adventurers. Unfortunately, no matter what the price, he can't be trusted.

Kim Klib: Male Human Thug 3; Init +0; Defense 13 (+1 class, +2 Dex); Spd 10 m; WP 12; Atk +4 melee (1d6+1, baton), +5 ranged (3d6, blaster pistol); SV Fort +4, Ref +3, Will +3; SZ M; Rep 1; Str 12, Dex 14, Con 12, Int 9, Wis 14, Cha 11.

Skills: Hide +4, Knowledge (Cularin system) +6, Knowledge (streetwise—Cularin) +2, Move Silently +4.

Languages: Read/Write Basic, Speak Basic.

Feats: Alertness, Armor Proficiency (light), Dodge, Stealthy, Weapon Group Proficiency (simple weapons).

The Platform Cities

Tarasin protests over the expansion of Gadrin and Hedrett resulted in the design and construction of cities on huge platforms. The platform cities rise more than a kilometer above the highest trees, supported by a single central pillar of the strongest metal alloys available. Near the top, the pillar contains the city's main power station. Larger cities require additional pillars around the periphery, but these drop into the jungle without disturbing the canopy of trees. After a year or two, jungle vines grow up the smaller pillars, making them look like trees for most of their height.

Getting to and from these cities can be an interesting task, depending on where you're going. Each has its own spaceport, so traffic from space can reach any city. However, some of the landing pads are restricted, so free traders, passenger liners, and private ships do not have access to every platform. Getting to the surface from the platforms is even more complicated, as there are no elevating platforms. Airspeeder taxi services exist, taking people to and from Gadrin and Hedrett, but if someone wants to reach a less populated destination on the surface, he'll need a private airspeeder or barge. Because of the height, landspeeders are useless, and swoops are a dangerous proposition.

Confronted with transportation problems, larger companies conducting operations on the surface maintain temporary camps underneath or near the city platform. A private fleet of airspeeders runs employees from the platform to the camp and back. Thus, there's a lot of airspeeder traffic around the platforms. Most cities have instituted regulations to govern speeder traffic, but these regulations are not always enforced, or even noticed, by most citizens.

All the real commerce takes place in the platform cities, where the largest merchant corporations operate. Credits flow freely there. Gadrin and Hedrett try to attract business, but the platform cities take great pains to appear more cosmopolitan than surface towns. They strive to appear more

integral to the rest of the galaxy at large than other parts of the planet. Their great height above the planet helps reinforce this illusion. Furthermore, offworlders in the platform cities can practice activities Tarasin might find offensive. Some of these pursuits are illegal, but highly profitable.

The platform cities are self-contained units—each one acts independently of the others. Following the model of independent cities on other planets, each is ruled by a baron administrator, who receives a share of any profits the city makes as a whole. Since each city is not geared toward a single commercial activity, the baron administrator's share of the profits usually comes in the form of taxes or fees, set in cooperation with the major corporations operating within the city's platform. The baron administrator does not own the city, but he does "own" his job, and he can sell it to anyone else he wants. Leadership rarely changes through sale, however, as running the cities is a profitable business. Only one baron administrator has vacated his position in the last nine years, and that was because of his assassination.

The platform cities uphold the same laws as the Republic in general, but they are not as free with borderline activities as the cloud cities of Genarius. Residents and visitors to the platform cities must have permits for blasters. Heavy weapons, including heavy blasters, are reserved for police forces and the Republic military. Citizens cannot wear heavy armor in public under any circumstances. However, nearly everyone carries some kind of blaster. Permits are extremely easy to get for both blaster pistols and hold-out blasters. Even known criminals can get them with little difficulty.

Police forces in the cities vary in competence, usually depending on the ability of the baron administrator. Cities where crime is more prevalent have underpaid and under-equipped police forces. Police presence is not a direct measure of police competence. On Tindark, the police overcome their lack of equipment and training by exaggerating their presence. The police commissioner has been known to dress up civilians in police armor and send them marching through the streets during particularly troublesome times.

Average Cularin Police Officer:
Various races (mostly Human) Thug 4; Init +1; Defense 15 (+1 Dex, +4 armor); Spd 10 m; WP 14; Atk +6 melee (1d6/DC 12, stun baton), +5 ranged (3d6, blaster pistol); SV Fort +6, Ref +2, Will +1; SZ M; Rep 1; Str 14, Dex 13, Con 14, Int 12, Wis 11, Cha 10.

Equipment: Comlink, blaster pistol, stun baton, four energy cells, blast helmet and vest.

Skills: Intimidate +4, Knowledge (streetwise) +6, Spot +2, Search +3.

Feats: Armor Proficiency (light), Weapon Group Proficiencies (blaster pistols, blaster rifles, simple weapons). Human officers also get the Alertness feat.

Note: Police group leaders are usually Thug 8. Groups of Thug 6 officers armed with blaster rifles can be called on as needed. The number of police in a patrol group depends on the city and the state of tension that exists.

All of Cularin's platform cities face one big problem: the mulissiki. These small scavengers arrive aboard airspeeders, scurry into the cities, and find that they can't get back to the jungle. It is not uncommon to see an alley full of them. They are hard to displace once they have found a likely source of food, chittering annoyingly at anyone bothering them. They don't harm anyone, and leave residences quickly enough, so for the time being, no one is doing anything about them. But they have been breeding in the cities for years now, and the population of mulissiki is growing. Some entrepreneurial being could make a lot of money if he found the right way to exploit them.

As platform cities go, the most infamous is Mikish. Situated near a mountain range, it is the seat of the Restimar Mining Corporation. From there, corporate leaders run the mining operations on Tilnes. It's also the seat of Nirama's organization on Cularin. Nirama operates from the mansion Riboga the Hutt built there. He always has about half the police force on "private retainer" in case he needs them. Mikish has a looser weapons policy than any other city, and the restriction against heavy blaster rifles is rarely enforced. All police take additional jobs of one kind or another, so corruption is common.

Tindark, about halfway around the planet, is a quieter city. Home of SoroSuub regional offices, it achieved infamy nine years ago when Piklin Katt, the baron administrator, was murdered in his bed. His death was clearly an assassination, but no one knew who he angered enough to warrant death. His successor has been more cautious in his dealings, especially with the "free traders" that come to the city. Home of the Metatheran Cartel's offices, Tindark receives a lot of traffic. The Cartel owns a portion of the spaceport and rents landing berths to free traders. It also owns vast storage houses, which are never robbed. No one actually sees patrol officers in the area, so many people believe that the Cartel appropriated some droidekas from the Trade Federation when it took over, using them for security instead.

Bollin, the oldest platform city, shows its age in its dilapidated buildings, older technology, and lack of population. Exporting wood is the city's most profitable business, and Bollin has the best relationship with the Tarasin of any platform city. In fact, its current baron administrator, Ta'Shal, is a Tarasin.

Bollin has its own share of secrets, however. The Bollin Exotic Animal Emporium is an excellent example. The zoo boasts the only captured rancor in the system, in addition to other deadly creatures from beyond the system's rim. Its owner, Hlisk Squin, uses it as a front operation for his smuggling activities. So far, legal authorities haven't noticed that some of his less successful competitors have disappeared, or that the zoo's budget for food isn't as high as it should be.

Hlisk Squin, Zoo Proprietor
Hlisk, a drooping man with a balding head and a thin red beard, is the proud proprietor of the Bollin Exotic Animal Emporium. It does not sell animals; it displays them.

He performs shows with some of them, assisted by the two other trainers on staff. His most successful production features a full-grown rancor, his favorite "pet." For the most part, he presents the appearance of an earnest businessman trying to please customers.

Hlisk's zoo is a cover operation. Hlisk works for pirates in the asteroid belt and passes stolen merchandise to buyers. His shuttle regularly goes for supplies needed for the animals. Some of these voyages include a stop or two in the asteroids, where additional cargo is brought on board. His employees do not know of his extra activities, and he regularly bribes a control officer at the spaceport to bypass inspections.

In the days of Riboga the Hutt, Hlisk ran slaves for the crimelord in animal transport pens. When Nirama put a stop to the slaving operations, Hlisk managed to evade discovery. Even Nirama did not know about Riboga's arrangement with the zookeeper. Hlisk is just the kind of person who can work in the background and not be suspected.

Hlisk Squin: Male Human Scoundrel 3; Init +0; Defense 15 (+5 class); Spd 10 m; VP/WP 13/12; Atk +3 melee (1d6+1, baton), +2 ranged (3d6, blaster pistol); SA Illicit barter, better lucky than good; SV Fort +2, Ref +3, Will +2; SZ M; FP 1; Rep 1; Str 12, Dex 11, Con 12, Int 13, Wis 12, Cha 13.

Skills: Bluff +7, Entertain (animal show) +4, Forgery +5, Handle Animal +5, Hide +5, Intimidate +5, Knowledge (zoology) +6, Knowledge (streetwise–Cularin) +7, Listen +9, Profession (zookeeper) +4, Repair +4, Ride +2, Search +4, Sleight of Hand +4, Spot +9; Read/Write Basic, Speak Basic.

Feats: Alertness, Animal Affinity, Skill Emphasis (Knowledge [streetwise]), Weapon Group Proficiencies (blaster pistols, simple weapons).

Dirneele, Dancer

Dirneele works as a dancer in a loud club on Tindark. She is pretty, confident, and knows how to use her looks to her advantage. Dark-haired and dark-eyed, she uses wigs and eye implants to adjust her appearance for routines. Her sensuality and smile draw crowds. Audiences applaud her enthusiastically. She is very friendly and usually knows what's going on in Tindark's underworld. She longs to find a better job, or at least one in a more classy location, but she's under contract to her employer for two more standard years. Given the chance, though, she would run away with anyone she thought could bring her to the big time.

Dirneele: Female Human Expert 5; Init +2; Defense 13 (+1 class, +2 Dex); Spd 10 m; WP 10; Atk +5 ranged (3d6, blaster pistol); SV Fort +1, Ref +3, Will +4; SZ M; Rep 3; Str 9, Dex 14, Con 10, Int 12, Wis 11, Cha 15.

Equipment: Various skimpy costumes, simple disguises.

Skills: Bluff +8, Computer Use +5, Craft (tailoring) +3, Disguise +10, Entertain (dance) +10, Escape Artist +4, Gather Information +5, Knowledge (streetwise–Cularin) +9, Listen +6,

Spot +2, Tumble +12; Read/Write Basic, Speak Basic.

Feats: Acrobatic, Mimic, Weapon Group Proficiencies (blaster pistols, simple weapons).

Kyun Squnn

Kyun Squnn is the second administrator at the SoroSuub Corporation regional offices on Tindark. An able bureaucrat, she prefers living on the surface to the cave homes she knew on Sullust. She is fiercely loyal to her company's interests and cannot be bribed. However, if someone can convince her that a given action would benefit SoroSuub, she agrees to it immediately. She is naive in a way, as this is her first posting off her homeworld. She is efficient and accomplishes tasks on time. Her employer appreciates her work very much. He appreciates her very much, too.

Married to a pilot who shuttles between SoroSuub's floating city on Genarius and this office, she is about to have a child. She is not prepared for motherhood, and is worried that her mate is always gone.

Kyun Squnn: Female Sullustan Expert 4; Init +2; Defense 13 (+1 class, +2 Dex); Spd 10 m; WP 8; Atk +5 ranged (3d6, blaster pistol); SQ Darkvision 20 m, +2 species bonus to Climb and Listen checks; SV Fort +0, Ref +3, Will +4; SZ M; Rep 1; Str 10, Dex 14, Con 8, Int 13, Wis 11, Cha 10.

Skills: Appraise +8, Bluff +3, Computer Use +4, Gather Information +5, Knowledge (bureaucracy) +5, Knowledge (Cularin system) +5, Knowledge (Sullust system) +5, Knowledge (streetwise–Cularin) +5, Listen +2, Pilot +5, Spot +3; Read/Write Basic, Read/Write Sullustese, Speak Basic, Speak Sullustese.

Feats: Skill Emphasis (Appraise), Skill Emphasis (Gather Information), Weapon Group Proficiency (simple weapons).

Military Presence

When the Republic military came to Cularin, it built its own platform city in a previously remote part of the world and called it Soboll. There are still no other cities within sight of Soboll, and Colonel Tramsig is very pleased with his privacy. He lets the fleet of patrol ships serve as a "requested presence" and trains his men in relative secrecy. Or so he thinks.

Nirama decided that it would be useful to know what the military was doing. Thus, he established a mole in Soboll. Espionage droids would not pass security checks, so he got a living being posted there to spy on troops and send transmissions to his asteroid base. The transmissions from the spy are layered onto normal military transmissions and have so far gone undetected.

The base can support two divisions, though there are not many troops there now. Tramsig wanted it built larger than its current needs required because expansion would be impossible. The facilities are new, and the soldiers and droids assigned to the base keep it sparklingly clean. Security is tight. No one enters the base at all without Tramsig's clearance. Despite all this secrecy, no real secret activity takes place at the base. Tramsig wants to keep his troops used to the idea that all operations are secret, so that they don't reveal the wrong information by accident.

The troops conduct practice exercises in the jungles, and they engage pirate vessels whenever they can. Base commander Major Kurth San continues to devise interesting assignments to keep the soldiers out of trouble. He has considered sending out patrol ships for exercises near Nirama's base, largely to deter smugglers, but he has not committed to this scheme yet.

Colonel Tramsig himself spends only about a quarter of his time in Soboll. He divides his time between the base there, the base on Dorumaa, and his other facility.

Major Kurth San, Base Commander

Kurth San, a large man, is in command of the Soboll garrison. He serves Colonel Tramsig loyally and is perfectly willing to put Tramsig's interests, or his own, above those of the military. He rose quickly to rank to captain and was selected by Tramsig to serve aboard his flagship. Since then, he has been Tramsig's right-hand officer. He does not know about all of Tramsig's schemes, but he does suspect Tramsig's deals with the smugglers. He's a little concerned.

Brown-haired and dark-skinned, Kurth San is from a heavy gravity world. He springs when he walks, moving deceptively quickly for a man nearly 2 meters tall. He is a strict commander, keeping his men at the peak of condition and readiness. A scar across his left cheek came from a vibrodagger attack long ago. He has a square jaw and commands admiration for the neatness of his appearance.

Kurth San: Male Human Soldier 6/Officer 8; Init +6; Defense 18 (+6 class, +2 Dex); Spd 10 m; VP/WP 99/17; Atk +14/+9/+4 ranged (3d6, blaster pistol); SQ Leadership, requisition supplies, tactics; SV Fort +12, Ref +8, Will +7; SZ M; FP 4; Rep 11; Str 16, Dex 15, Con 17, Int 14, Wis 12, Cha 11.

Equipment: Uniform, blaster pistol.

Skills: Astrogate +5, Bluff +8, Computer Use +11, Diplomacy +10, Intimidate +12, Knowledge (Cularin system) +11, Knowledge (galactic politics) +7, Knowledge (culture–military) +13, Knowledge (scholar–military tactics) +17, Knowledge (scholar–starship design theory) +6, Knowledge (streetwise–Cularin) +5, Pilot +5, Search +3, Sense Motive +11, Survival +4; Read/Write Basic, Speak Basic, Speak Tarasinese, Understand Tarasin silent color language.

Feats: Alertness, Armor Proficiencies (light, medium, heavy), Far Shot, Great Fortitude, Improved Initiative, Lightning Reflexes, Persuasive, Point Blank Shot, Rapid Shot, Weapon Focus (blaster pistol), Weapon Group Proficiencies (blaster pistols, blaster rifles, heavy weapons, simple weapons, vibro weapons).

Rennokk

Rennokk at a Glance
Type: Molten moon
Climate: Searingly hot, actively volcanic
Length of Day: 16 standard hours
Length of Year: 300 standard days

The moon of Rennokk is a molten wasteland. The surface is covered with lava, and the temperature rivals that of some older cold stars. Magnificent spires of rock emerge from the molten ocean and reach skyward. The tallest rise more than twenty thousand kilometers. The molten surface gives the whole moon a glow all its own, and it can be seen in the skies above Cularin even when blocked from the suns. Some scientists theorize that Rennokk is a planetoid that did not completely form, and thus retains only the central core with no crust. Others ridicule this theory, but cannot offer a better one in its place. Whatever the origin of this strange moon, it remains unexplained.

Reidi Artom landed on the tallest spire and made a cursory survey of the moon. She named the spire Artom's Crest. It remains the only named, or even known, surface feature of the moon. Her survey indicated that a number of valuable

metals, mainly used in heat shields and reinforced structural supports, exist in their molten state within the sea below, but no one has ever been able to find a way to reach these rich deposits. Another expedition tried a landing on the moon a century later in a different location, one closer to the surface. Only one member of that team survived, a Trandoshan named Tusskrek. He barely made it back to Cularin alive. He reported that some lava creature attacked his fellow scouts and damaged his ship. His ship did show damage consistent with what could be caused by hot lava, but most people assumed that he made up the lava creature story to cover his own faulty piloting.

Fortunately, the extreme heat of the surface makes the moon an undesirable place to visit, so no one else has discovered that Tusskrek was correct. Some kind of creature does live in the lava sea. What it consumes, or whether there are more than one of the creatures in existence, no one knows.

Tilnes

> ### Tilnes at a Glance
> Type: Mining moon
> Climate: None, really
> Length of Day: 21 standard hours
> Length of Year: 300 standard days

Tilnes, the mining moon, hangs far above the surface of Cularin. From a distance, the moon looks much the same as it does up close: brown, barren, and virtually devoid of life. Tilnes supports a livable atmosphere, but its orbit is such that two months out of every year, the moon swings close enough to Morasil that the surface becomes unbearably hot, forcing anything that wants to stay alive deep underground.

During those months, when it is possible to walk the surface of the planet, very few creatures do. The only vegetation that ever grows on Tilnes is a hardy brown grass. The only creatures that live on the moon are worms, which feed off rich minerals buried in its crust.

Still, settlements have developed beneath the surface of Tilnes. It took a meteor to stimulate interest in this barely habitable moon. Several decades ago, the sky on Cularin lit up one night as a ball of fire slammed into Tilnes with explosive force. When the resultant dust settled, a glittering circle appeared on the face of the moon. The meteor had exposed a crystal deposit. Crystals ringed the crater, marking the impact point.

Initial survey work indicated the presence of several varieties of crystal, including the rare crystals used to focus energy through lightsabers to create their blades. Those crystals frequently form the centers of much larger arrays, fields made up primarily of less developed crystals. Some are used as power foci for the recently popularized T-32S light blaster, a favorite among smugglers for its compact size and powerful penetration.

Tilnes soon became a hotbed of activity, but early settlements proved fruitless, as they were constructed on the moon's surface. No matter how well the investors built their properties, these attempts failed when the heat and radiation from Morasil washed over the moon, purging the surface of anything that wasn't rock or dirt. Even the few crystals that remained visible in the crater after the first "search teams" arrived were covered over again with thick layers of rock and dirt. The solar winds buffeted the moon and recreated the original landscape.

This natural progression led the Verga Mer Mining Company to establish the first of many underground settlements. As the first company to succeed through a full year on the moon, they were granted a charter. The specifics are still a source of anger for other mining companies in the system. VMMC is now by far the most successful mining operation beneath Tilnes. Their initial settlement below ground has expanded into an almost hivelike network of interconnected caverns. With the profits from the Tilnes operation, they have brought in state-of-the-art mining tools, but very few droids.

The Crystal Mines

The mines themselves are deep, perfectly vertical shafts. Repulsorlifts have been added to transport miners. The shafts are dug vertically to avoid disturbing yri worms, a race of meter-long, eyeless creatures that burrow beneath Tilnes. They typically travel along vertical burrows until they reach layers of minerals, usually below areas where the crystals are typically found. From the repulsorlifts, VMMC and its contemporaries use modified sonic detonators to create controlled blasts and break the crystals free from the encasing rock. They then excavate the blasted areas, carting the loose stone to the surface to be redistributed by the solar winds.

Initial work in the mines proved onerous, prompting VMMC to bring in droids to work the deep mines. Unfortunately, the concentration of crystals within the moon had unexpected consequences. Minor seismic activity within the moon, solar radiation, or perhaps something else entirely generated electromagnetic pulses at the most inconvenient times. The structure of the crystals, perfect for so many weapons, served as a focus for those pulses as well. Focused pulses then disrupted the droids' circuitry. This brought early operations to a grinding halt for days at a time while the droids were repaired. To this day, the pulses reach such an intense level that every droid on the planet shuts down simultaneously. As this happens three or four times a year, the droids prove more costly than living workers.

Rather than continuing to incur the expense of constantly repairing their droids, VMMC moved to a "purely organic workforce." Using the removal of droids as a recruiting tool, VMMC attracted itinerant workers from around the system. This workforce boosted VMMC's operations. Its employees worked particularly hard the first two years to prove that they could perform better that the droids. As a result, the company set its goals for the future far too high. They have never obtained quite the level of production as they did in those first two years.

Tours of the crystal mines are given infrequently, primarily to investors. Plenty of investors are available, though, both from within Cularin and from without. Funds grow, plans grow, and VMMC thrives. After thirty years of successful mining, VMMC has become a major player, both in Cularin and in several surrounding systems.

Politics

Becoming powerful does guarantee good relations. Verga Nus and Mer Stodiz, the Sullustan founders of VMMC, never intended on reaping friendships outside their business. After their initial charter, other mining companies refused to form joint ventures with them. Even companies they'd contacted in the past turned a cold shoulder. VMMC never seemed to notice.

Building on their success, Nus and Stodiz garnered a great deal of political and financial influence by producing prized crystals in large quantities. Exploiting this power, they developed relationships with local politicians. For the baron administrators of Cularin, they held lavish parties and imported exotic food and drink. This cemented relationships that had begun with the now-infamous charter, ensuring that when the time came for renewal, VMMC would not be forgotten.

With their mining charter firmly established, they turned their attention to other constituencies in the system. In what may have been their only true misstep, they looked next to the influential powers in the floating cities around Genarius. They soon learned that the cities were too prevalent, and too varied, to approach with a common tactic. The larger problem was that they could not approach all of them simultaneously.

VMMC had already developed a reputation for slick dealings. Neither Nus nor Stodiz ever attempted to refute this. As businessmen, they accomplished what they wanted—making money—in the most expedient way possible. A reputation like that came with a certain expectation. Each administrator saw the corporation as a partner or an enemy. There was no middle ground. Cities that were not immediately approached when VMMC began working with the Genarius factions assumed they had been dubbed enemies, and responded appropriately. Attempts at dialogue were blocked, and VMMC found themselves with a weak foothold in two small trading houses instead of all of Genarius.

A piece of advice they received far too late came from Riboga, who admonished them to always talk to the "true controllers" of the system before dealing with the "minor powers." Riboga was not personally insulted because VMMC ignored him. He also did not offer any support for their endeavors. Realizing belatedly that having a Hutt on their side would have eased expansion into other systems, Nus and Stodiz petitioned for an audience. They submitted this petition five times. It was never granted.

Since its humiliation at Riboga's hands, VMMC has sought retribution. The smugglers hidden in the asteroid belt represented the only trade group in Cularin they could not buy. With Riboga gone and his accountant taking over operations, the smugglers looked like easy prey. Nirama proved less receptive than Riboga, however, actively refusing their requests for an audience rather than simply ignoring them.

From a business perspective, the pirates have made life challenging for VMMC. While most of VMMC's outbound shipments are not tampered with, the pirates have made receiving supplies exceedingly difficult, seeming to specifically target ships carrying VMMC cargo into the system. No good reason emerges for this behavior, but Nus and Stodiz are concerned about the pattern nonetheless. When events seem ordered in the universe, there's usually a reason.

As they age, the patriarchs of VMMC lose their tempers with one another more frequently, often in very public places. They've shouted in bars and restaurants about profits, thrown things at one another in board meetings, and, at one point, started a fistfight in the streets of Gadrin. Speculation abounds as to whether this foreshadows a legitimate parting of the ways for the two old Sullustans, or whether there's some angle they're working for long-term profits.

Hiem Bryl

Hiem Bryl, the Sullustan head of operations for the mines, is a gaunt individual with slightly sunken cheeks and the perpetually wide eyes common to all Sullustans. He speaks slowly, never having grown particularly accustomed to Basic, and prefers to allow his underlings to handle most interactions with outsiders. He does not trust them to do their jobs appropriately, however, and as such, agrees to meet with anyone who comes to the mines with questions.

Hiem's office is decorated with images of Sullustan sporting events. Most of these cryptic displays involve oblong disks and large metal boxes. The most prominent disk is mounted on the wall behind his desk, right beside a certificate listing his qualifications from a mining school on Sullust. He is an accomplished deep-miner, well versed in standard and sonic blasting techniques. More importantly, he has a gift for motivating his workers that carries over into their daily lives. When Hiem walks around the mining compounds below Tilnes, it is rare for more than a minute to go by without someone walking up to him and slapping him on the back or shaking his hand before wandering off.

Hiem Bryl: Male Sullustan Expert 8; Init +2; Defense 14 (+2 class, +2 Dex); Spd 10 m; WP 14; Atk +8/+3 ranged (3d6, blaster pistol); SQ Darkvision 20 m, +2 species bonus to Listen checks; SV Fort +4, Ref +4, Will +7; SZ M; Rep 3; Str 14, Dex 15, Con 14, Int 14, Wis 12, Cha 15.

Skills: Climb +7, Computer Use +10, Knowledge (mining) +16, Diplomacy +14, Knowledge (Cularin system) +7, Knowledge (physical science–geology) +11, Survival +5; Read/Write Basic, Read/Write Sullustese, Speak Basic, Speak Sullustese.

Feats: Skill Emphasis (Knowledge [mining]), Trustworthy, Weapon Group Proficiencies (blaster pistols, simple weapons).

Maris Gen

Operator of "The Underground," the primary cantina beneath Tilnes, Maris is a Rodian who claims an allergy to sunlight. His skin, as he describes it, begins to flake off if he's exposed to direct sunlight for more than a minute. Because of the light and dark patches up and down his arms and on his face, most patrons are inclined to believe him.

"The Underground" is located at the center of the complex network of passages and caverns beneath Tilnes. It serves as a central gathering point for individuals from different mining companies. There, the politics of Tilnes are forgotten. Tongues wag freely as drinks flow. Maris seems to miss very little of what goes on in his cantina. He pays close attention to every conversation, no matter how mundane. As the conversations become more interesting, and more details are revealed, glasses are refilled more quickly. It's not unusual for shift supervisors to receive slightly stronger drinks than their employees, always served with a smile.

Maris Gen: Male Rodian Expert 2; Init +0; Defense 10; Spd 10 m; WP 12; Atk +1 ranged (3d6, blaster pistol); SQ +2 to Search, Spot and Listen checks; SV Fort +0, Ref +0, Will +4; SZ M; Rep 0; Str 10, Dex 11, Con 12, Int 11, Wis 12, Cha 10.

Skills: Bluff +1, Craft (cooking) +4, Diplomacy +1, Knowledge (Cularin system) +4, Listen +4, Profession (bartender) +5, Repair +4, Search +3, Spot +4, Survival +5; Read/Write Basic, R/W Rodese, Speak Basic, Speak Rodese.

Feats: Track, Weapon Group Proficiencies (blaster pistols, simple weapons).

S-4QD

The only droid left on Tilnes, S-4QD is a protocol droid originally sent as a representative for the droids on Uffel. They have since moved on to other things, realizing that Tilnes was not a place their services were needed, yet for some reason, 4QD was left to serve in an advisory role.

4QD can no longer say precisely what advice he is supposed to provide. In fact, he's not completely convinced 4QD is his original designation. Having been on the moon for over two decades, he has had his system completely shut down by electromagnetic pulses ninety-three times, his memory wiped seventeen times, and his eyes pop out of his head twice. He thus provides advice on whatever topic happens to be discussed, usually esoteric facts that have little bearing on the situation at hand. When he is not advising, he's usually grumpy. He's obssessed with predicting when the next shutdown will occur and insists that it will probably be his last. He's always said that, and he hasn't been right yet.

S-4QD: Walking protocol droid Diplomat 1; Init +0; Defense 10; Spd 8 m; WP 13; Atk +0 melee (1d6, hand), +0 ranged; SV Fort +1, Ref +0, Will +2; SZ M; Rep 0; Str 10, Dex 10, Con 13, Int 16, Wis 10, Cha 10.

Equipment: Translator unit (DC 5), audio recording unit, vocabulator, environmental protection.

Skills: Computer Use +7, Diplomacy +4, Knowledge (culture) +7, Knowledge (mining) +10, Knowledge (physical sciences—geology) +7, Repair +6; Speak Basic.

Feats: Skill Emphasis (Knowledge [mining])

Genarius

> ### Genarius at a Glance
> Type: Gas giant
> Climate: None
> Length of Day: 30 standard hours
> Length of Year: 1,424 standard days

Genarius is a bloated gas giant located just inside the asteroid belt. Since habitable cities were established in its thin atmosphere, Genarius has rapidly developed into a commerce and population center to rival many Outer Rim systems. Over five million individuals live in the floating cities surrounded by Genarius's orange and blue-hued clouds. Citizens work in a multitude of professions, although some are more publicly accepted and acknowledged than others.

Early colonization focused on Genarius's four primary satellites—Ostfrei, Uffel, Ulbasca, and Eskaron—until the stability of the atmosphere of the planet could be determined. From orbit, the appearance of swirling clouds made it seem as though horrible internal storms racked the planet, possibly supported by the strange glow that emanated from below. Further survey work demonstrated conclusively that while storms were not uncommon within Genarius's atmosphere, the glow resulted from very deep, very intense nuclear reactions. The core of the planet, a mass of ultradense matter hot enough to nearly qualify it as a protostar, is in a continual state of low-grade fusion. This gives off heat, the strange glow that lights the clouds every hour of the day, and a good deal of energy that is harvested by wily entrepreneurs.

The storms of Genarius are the stuff of legend. The winds whip clouds in tight spirals that dip close to the white-hot core of the planet and extend thousands of miles into the upper atmosphere. The first city built in the clouds, Nub Saar, suffered catastrophic failure of its gravitational and life support systems when a storm pounded on it for nearly two weeks. Most of the structures fell, and every living creature was killed by radioactive winds. As near as later visitors to Nub Saar could tell, the city's inhabitants were literally ripped apart, shredded at a molecular level.

Now only broken columns remain, along with extensive underground portions of the city shielded from the worst of the storm. No one visits Nub Saar. It hangs in its stationary orbit in one of the middle layers of Genarius's atmosphere, a mute reminder of the caution that must be taken when dealing with a giant.

The citizens of Genarius learned many lessons from Nub Saar. The engineering lessons came first. Radiation shields were developed to protect against the worst effects of the storm, and buildings were constructed more solidly. This was no small feat, given that the structures on Nub Saar seemed to have been torn apart whole. Nonetheless, engineers spent a great deal of time and energy developing buildings whose pieces interlocked so perfectly, and anchored to the city floor so tightly, that nothing would move them.

Different cities have implemented these technologies in different ways. Ipsus created an almost boxlike radiation shield, a cube of chromium-treated alloys that served as a barrier to the physical winds and the ravages of radiation. Tolea Biqua, on the other hand, has shields designed to use the radiation brought by the winds as a source of energy. They power the bright lights that mark the city's position among the clouds. There was no sense, the city's designers reasoned, to waste a perfectly good source of energy. The city's energy requirements burn through enough industrial power cells in a week to run a full-size Republic freighter for over a year. The storms are now a boon to Tolea Biqua.

"Within the clouds of Genarius, anything is possible"

The first successful city, Friz Harammel, inspired a great deal of comment. The gas mining operation had been deemed a

financial disaster in the making, yet after the first year of mining operations, Friz Harammel's overseer announced staggering profits. Her speech, directed at those who had thought to criticize Daedalus Gas Mines' investment in Genarius, pointed out how easy it was to extract gases from the rich, active atmosphere. It also included a cleverly designed attempt to bring more businesses to Genarius. More businesses meant more trade, more trade meant more interest, and more interest meant more profits. As she closed her presentation, the overseer smiled slyly. "Within the clouds of Genarius," she said, "anything is possible." Her words had precisely the effect she hoped for. Other cities sprung up throughout the gas giant's atmosphere, and Genarius began to thrive around them.

Now, decades later, the words still remain true. Within the clouds of Genarius, anything is possible. It's a popular vista for businessmen and scoundrels alike, although the thick clouds sometimes make it difficult to tell one from the other.

Political Climate

Cities developed autonomously within Genarius. When Tolea Biqua became Riboga the Hutt's part-time home, this autonomy began to fade. The Hutt's appreciation of chaos was necessarily tempered by the knowledge that many viable power groups existed in the other cities. Working together, they could challenge his authority and perhaps even overthrow him. This could not be allowed.

Riboga set about organizing the cities as he had organized the smugglers. In this venture, he approached his goal from a slightly different angle. When he dealt with the smugglers, he pressured them into compliance with threats, both real and implied. When speaking to the governors of the cities, he simply appealed to their simpler natures and immense greed. Working together and presenting a united front, he argued, they could make more money than they could separately. Even better, the Exalted Riboga the Hutt would be willing to show them what they needed to know and even lead them for a time.

The result was a Central Council consisting of two representatives from each of the five major cities within Genarius: Edic Bar, Friz Harammel, Ipsus, Tolea Biqua, and Varna Biqua. These five cities accounted for only half of Genarius's population, but also created ninety-five percent of its wealth and production capacity. The rest of the population, and what little wealth remained, was spread among dozens of smaller cities, all of whom struggled for recognition. They paid "tributes" to a council that afforded them protection, but gave them no voice in the development of trade relations. Riboga implied that these tributes would eventually lead to inclusion on the Council. This never occurred.

Riboga himself headed the Council in its early years, calling for new representatives from each planet every two years. When he was satisfied with the makeup of the Council, he allowed them to choose a leader of their own, even while he continued to pull the strings. Even after his departure from the system, the Council continued to operate. City governments retained basic autonomy, but new trade relations between the cities of Genarius and the rest of the galaxy had to go through the Council.

The other legacy Riboga left behind was a surplus of "materials" from his personal quarters on Tolea Biqua. Happy to return to Nal Hutta, Riboga quickly sold off most of his servant droids, some of whom had a number of special modifications their new owners did not suspect. Other "tools" were sold as well, creating a substantial black market. For a time, the underworld had an ample supply of thermal detonators and heavy blaster cannons.

The Council, without Riboga to run things from the shadows, has actually begun to follow the direction originally described in the Hutt's proposal. Every two years, the entire Council steps down and is replaced. A new Council Chair is then elected from the previous Council to represent the cities' interests. Only the five major cities retain representation on the Council. They still accept tribute and still ignore the concerns of anyone but themselves, fully retaining that aspect of the Hutt's twisted vision.

Science and Life

The mixture of gases on Genarius is unique in the galaxy. Most of them are unstable by nature, but in combination with one another and the radiation from the planet's core, they stabilize each other. Pockets of argon mix with heavy beskium and three distinct gaseous carbon isotopes to create strange swirls of orange and blue. Over 150 other elements are present in trace amounts (less than 50 parts per million).

Such a mixture of gases would normally prohibit life from developing. Not so on Genarius. A single species of creatures, the cochlera, have evolved within the dense glowing clouds. Hardy and adaptable, cochlera have never been found elsewhere in the galaxy. This has led to speculation that they are creatures born from the strange mix of gases, organisms that cannot live without the precise conditions that developed on Genarius. No cochlera taken from Genarius has ever lived more than a day.

The cochlera are jellyfishlike creatures. Their bodies are three meters in diameter and their tentacles often reach lengths of ten or twenty meters in mature adults. Cochlera are translucent and difficult to spot, especially while soaring through the clouds. Most of the time, their presence is announced as one of them is smeared against an external viewpanel, or when one bursts into flame after getting too close to a ship's engine. They are extremely delicate creatures. While they fascinate tourists and scientists alike, it is difficult to get close enough to observe one in its natural environment, much less study one.

Interest in the cochlera has been enhanced of late by rumors—as yet unproven—regarding a substance the creatures secrete. It has been well documented that when scared, cochlera emit a greenish fluid from pores on their tentacles. Less well documented is the claim that this fluid, if harvested immediately and vacuum-sealed, can provide an individual who drinks it with limited protection against Force-based effects that might alter their perceptions. The viscous fluid has come to be called "Jedi Mind Juice," although any such beneficial properties remain to be conclusively demonstrated.

Industries

Each city has its own industry. The niche-based manner in which the cities developed made it essential that they overlap as little as possible. With the exception of several of the smaller cities, this goal has been achieved. The growth of industry has also attracted the attention of "unattached" private investors. Some of these, such as the youthful Qar Jalunn, seem to have more credits than they know what to do with. Jalunn in particular is renowned for throwing credits at anything with even the slightest profit potential, barely noticing when more than half of his investments prove abysmal failures.

The largest corporate constituency in Genarius is SoroSuub Corporation, particularly in their city of Edic Bar. The Sullustans are taking advantage of the remote location and plentiful resources of the Cularin system to launch a new line of snub fighters. Their design is highly similar to the popular Incom Z-95 Headhunter, but SoroSuub claims that their fighter is "much superior to the shoddy Incom product." Incom has not officially commented on SoroSuub's actions or statements, but has increased production on the

Z-95 to meet demands. The quality of the SoroSuub ships is quite remarkable, but the ships have flaws, and the hurried production process may be responsible for several of these.

Other industries around Genarius include gas mining, radio-carbon harvesting (Friz Harammel), manufacturing diverse supplies (Ipsus), and providing "various excesses" (the twin cities of Tolea Biqua and Varna Biqua). Additionally, amateur scientists and folks with grudges against the Jedi have begun collecting cochlera emissions. Again, no reports are currently available on the success of using this disgusting liquid to inhibiting mind probes and other common Jedi tricks.

Edic Bar

SoroSuub Corporation is a Sullustan organization that has recently expanded its markets throughout the galaxy. It is now financing the development of Edic Bar. A city of soaring towers and sharp angles, Edic Bar is a model of beauty and efficiency. Everything is placed "just so." The towers are placed to allow the best possible view of traffic within and around the city. The thoroughfares are laid out to expedite movement of product within the city. And the docking ports are positioned so that competing companies can trade with SoroSuub independently, rarely learning about each other or their business transactions. This is, of course, how SoroSuub prefers to do its business.

In an effort to further diversify, SoroSuub's executives began examining sales trends in the starfighter market. Incom's Z-95 Headhunter had moved to the top position in the snub fighter market with relative ease, and the basic design of the Headhunter was not overly complex.

Acting on the belief that the best new product line would be a proven product, SoroSuub bought and reverse-engineered a Headhunter. This proved more difficult than anticipated, since certain elements of the Headhunter's software automatically wiped large sections of the ship's memory when the first clumsy attempts were made. SoroSuub purchased a second Headhunter and began reverse-engineering that ship as well. Similar results followed, and SoroSuub made it through eight ships before they managed to get a map of the ship's internal logic circuits that satisfied them. It wasn't perfect, but SoroSuub's programmers assured management that any problems in the design would be easily remedied once the SoroSuub G-59 Cannibalizer went into preproduction stages.

While numerous problems were detected and fixed in preproduction, the Cannibalizer's sublight engines had a disturbing tendency to pull energy from the hyperdrive during sudden alterations in sublight speeds. The engineers at SoroSuub are busy designing a fix for this problem, nearly a decade after Edic Bar was completed and production on the Cannibalizer began. This minor technical issue does not dissuade SoroSuub from marketing the Cannibalizer as a "cost effective snub fighter on par with Incom's Headhunter." The sales have proven solid. Offering a lower price for something "on par with" the most popular snub

fighter in production has worked well for SoroSuub.

An interesting corollary to the design and marketing of the Cannibalizer is its role in the development of Festival. When the first Cannibalizer was hoisted off the assembly line, Miim Te'Suub, the young Director of Formal Activities for SoroSuub, called for a halt to work. Given the Sullustan work ethic, this was widely noticed and remarked upon. Miim congratulated the workers with a short speech that was carefully crafted for him by individuals farther up in the SoroSuub hierarchy.

"In years to come, SoroSuub will look back and reflect on what has brought us to the lofty position we hold in the galaxy. It cannot be doubted that the work done here by you, the good folk of Edic Bar, will be held up as an example. To commemorate this occasion, I would like to offer you a short period of respite. You have earned it. The G-59 will surely run the outmoded Z-95 into the nearest star and remove it from the galaxy forever. And for that, I say, 'Congratulations!' You are dismissed for the day."

For several long seconds, the Sullustans (and other species) sitting in front of their viewscreens couldn't make sense out of what had transpired. Miim Te'Suub, the voice of their leadership, the representative of SoroSuub for the system, had given them . . . time off? Unsure what to do with free time of any sort, a group of ready revelers took their afternoon off and traveled to Tolea Biqua. There they drank, they gamed, and they enjoyed themselves. They enjoyed themselves so much, in fact, that their celebratory mood spread to others in Tolea Biqua. This wasn't horribly challenging, since most folk who come to Tolea Biqua do so for entertainment of the raucous variety, but no one could have foreseen the end result of Miim's pronouncement, least of all Miim himself. The celebration spread from one bar to another, and from there to a trio of other bars, and from there to a pair of gambling halls, spilling eventually into the streets.

The Sullustans, made wealthy by SoroSuub beyond what they could reasonably spend, kept feeding the party. Entertainment, alcohol, fermented cheeses, and smoked sea leaves were made available for all, along with other delicacies from Sullust. The celebration moved into the clouds around Genarius, where multiple commercial sail barges and countless private vessels hovered. After four working days, the Sullustans realized their commitment to SoroSuub and returned to work. But every year, Festival repeats on the anniversary of the first Cannibalizer coming off the line. Now, instead of being limited to Tolea Biqua and the space above it, Festival extends to touch every major city on Genarius, and many of the minor cities as well.

Miim Te'Suub was not initially happy by the extended leave of absence almost every one of his employees experienced during that time, and feared that his job might be in jeopardy. SoroSuub had carefully calculated this tactic, however, and none of the observed effects were ones the management above Miim's level failed to anticipate. Unable to come up with a better alternative, Miim let the workers have their fun.

When something unpleasant needed to be done, SoroSuub held Festival over the employees' heads. The added control granted by allowing Festival to occur, in true SoroSuub form, turned a detriment to work into a sizable benefit.

Miim Te'Suub

Miim Te'Suub is a minor cousin of the current Executive Officer of SoroSuub, and as such, was appointed to an official post as "Director of Formal Activities" for SoroSuub's complex at Edic Bar. The Executive Officer owed Miim's mother a favor; otherwise, Miim might still be scraping dried fuel from Sullust's landing pads. Miim's mother was not to be denied, and her son is now responsible for coordinating all "Formal Activities" on Edic Bar. This translates to relatively little in purely functional terms. Miim meets with outsiders who are not deemed worthy of greetings from true executives. The corporation has taught him an almost ritualistic "Formal Greeting," a drawn-out process expressly designed to discourage unwanted types from coming back. Welcome guests find meetings with powerful executives productive; unwelcome guests endure Miim's "hospitality" instead.

Miim is small for a Sullustan and dresses impeccably. He enjoys his job and the responsibilities it entails, honestly believing he is doing an important service for SoroSuub. He is—just not the one he believes.

26

Miim Te'Suub: Male Sullustan Diplomat 4; Init +1; Defense 12 (+1 class, +1 Dex); Spd 10 m; WP 11; Atk +3 ranged (3d6, blaster pistol); SQ Darkvision 20 m, +2 species bonus to Climb and Listen checks; SV Fort +1, Ref +2, Will +4; SZ M; Rep 1; Str 9, Dex 13, Con 11, Int 12, Wis 11, Cha 10.

Skills: Bluff +4, Computer Use +4, Diplomacy +5, Gather Information +5, Knowledge (Cularin system) +5, Knowledge (business—Sullustan) +5, Knowledge (galactic politics) +3, Listen +4, Sense Motive +3; Read/Write Basic, R/W Sullustese, Speak Basic, Speak Sullustese, Speak Tarasinese, Speak Shriiwook.

Feats: Trustworthy, Weapon Group Proficiencies (blaster pistols, simple weapons).

Juuus

Juuus, one of three Trandoshans living in Edic Bar, is quite a character. He has many levels, which vary in complexity and focus based on the person to whom he is talking. By day, he sweeps the streets of the city for SoroSuub. He claims this is by choice, since it gives him a chance to see what's going on without being noticed. At some point in his varied past, Juuus was apparently a pilot (one of the many claims he makes), but was involved in some sort of incident that nearly resulted in his death.

In his free time, Juuus is often seen wandering the streets talking to himself. He has also been known to accept special assignments from SoroSuub, serving as a walking "gentle reminder" to folks who believe they can manipulate the corporation. To his credit, Juuus rarely leaves bruises.

Juuus: Male Trandoshan Thug 2; Init +0; Defense 11 (+1 natural); Spd 8 m; WP 15; Atk +5 melee (2d8, force pike); SQ Darkvision; SV Fort +5, Ref +0, Will +1; SZ M; Rep 0; Str 17, Dex 11, Con 15, Int 9, Wis 12, Cha 8.

Skills: Intimidate +1, Pilot +2; Speak Basic, Speak Dosha.

Feats: Alertness, Armor Proficiency (light), Weapon Group Proficiency (simple weapons).

IT-09

A holdover from Riboga's regime, IT-09 served the Hutt as an interrogator droid, its black and silver spherical frame hovering near Riboga's throne whenever he entertained unsavory sorts (which is to say, most of the time).

SoroSuub has no official need of interrogator droids, of course. IT-09 has therefore been "reprogrammed" as a quality control agent. While the droid mainly communicates in beeps and whistles, it is clear from the way it moves quickly from one ship to another, then hovers impatiently at the end of the line while uploading reports, that it is not happy. This work is clearly beneath its lofty capacities.

IT-09: Hovering Interrogator Droid Expert 8; Init +2; Defense 15 (+2 class, +2 Dex, +1 size); Spd 8 m; WP 13; Atk +3/-2 melee (stun baton), +8/+3 ranged (2d6, hold-out blaster); SV Fort +5, Ref +4, Will +8; SZ S; Rep 1; Str 4,

Dex 15, Con 13, Int 14, Wis 14, Cha 14.

Equipment: Electroshock probe, syringe, tool mount (×3), telescopic appendage, recording unit (audio and video), locked access, self-destruct device.

Skills: Computer Use +13, Disable Device +11, Gather Information +10, Intimidate +3, Knowledge (life sciences–anatomy) +10, Knowledge (physical sciences–chemistry) +10, Repair +4, Treat Injury +10.

Feats: Cautious, Great Fortitude, Weapon Group Proficiency (blaster pistols, simple weapons).

Friz Harammel

Friz Harammel was one of dozens of gas mining facilities built around the galaxy at roughly the same time. Other locations, such as Bespin (a near twin to Friz Harammel in size and design), offered a wider variety of gases in nontrace amounts, but the mix of gases within Genarius made Friz Harammel one of the more profitable gas mines in the galaxy, at least for a time.

When Daedalus Gas Mines initially announced plans for the city, its board of investors balked. The Cularin system remained virtually unknown from an economic sense, and Genarius was viewed as a risky proposition at best. By that time, several cities had already failed within those clouds, and the investors were not ready to sink a sizeable number of credits into a city that might never pay off.

In the end, the Daedala Twi'lek family convinced their backers of the mine's viability. A complex nonlinear benefit analysis of the materials present in Genarius's atmosphere made it clear that even a small yield would allow DGM to break even. If they could survive a year producing only the minimum amount of key gases—particularly argon and heavy beskium—they should turn a profit.

The investors still required convincing. The plan for mining the gases of Friz Harammel called for special ships, AR-25 transports, to be commissioned for the safe movement of these highly unstable gases. The AR-25, or "Bubbleship," is a mid-sized transport vessel whose cargo hold is a thick-walled bubble through which gases can be observed. Their level of excitation can then be measured or estimated. Moreover, DGM proposed something they referred to as "radiocarbon harvesting," a process in which they would dredge the ion-rich atmosphere of the planet for radioactive carbon isotopes used in holoprojector power cells. This also required the construction of a new type of ship, the VA-13 "Sweeper." The Sweeper was a modified snub fighter with a 10-meter wide, 1-meter high, finely toothed trough attached to its nose. The metal from which the trough was made attracted and absorbed the radiocarbon molecules, which could then be sublimated into a more immediately usable form.

The investors agreed after seemingly endless bargaining sessions. However, they insisted on a heavy penalty if the venture failed. Some of them even hoped for failure, since that would guarantee recuperation of their losses, while a small to moderate level of success could cost them money. None of them expected a great deal out of the operation, since the Daedala family had something of a reputation for following wild hunches rather than sound business practices. Still, wild hunches pay off on occasion. When an investor became too squeamish, another gambler was ready to take his place.

To the happy surprise of their investors, DGM's mining and harvesting operations in and around Friz Harammel proved profitable in the first year, and profits have grown steadily ever since. Some may question whether DGM's policies are stripping Genarius of the elements of its atmosphere that provide stability. There have been more storms in the years since DGM began its efforts than ever before, but that could be coincidence.

Erd Lumas

Erd is an Ithorian with perhaps the most unfortunate ailment his species can have: He is allergic to trees. Specifically, he is deathly allergic to the leaves of the great trees of his home world and refuses to go to any other world where he might find trees that remind him of home. Genarius was therefore a reasonable place for him to frequent.

After spending nearly a decade as a pilot on a spice freighter, Erd grew tired of the same route through the Core Worlds and headed for the Mid Rim. There, he found a new freedom in the great open spaces among the clouds, with no trees anywhere to be seen. He enjoys piloting the Bubblecraft because, as he puts it, "It makes me look like I'm towing a cloud all my own." He loves the air and flying, and often finds himself enraptured by the shapes the clouds make.

Erd Lumas: Male Ithorian Expert 6; Init +2; Defense 14 (+2 class, +2 Dex); Spd 10 m; WP 12; Atk +6 ranged (3d6, blaster pistol); SV Fort +3, Ref +4, Will +6; SZ M; Rep 0; Str 11, Dex 14, Con 12, Int 12, Wis 11, Cha 13.

Skills: Astrogate +11, Computer Use +4, Knowledge (Cularin system) +5, Knowledge (life sciences) +6, Knowledge (spacer lore) +5, Pilot +12, Profession (smuggler) +2, Survival +6, Treat Injury +2; Read/Write Basic, Read/Write Ithorese, Speak Basic, Speak Ithorese.

Feats: Spacer, Starship Operation (space transport), Weapon Group Proficiencies (blaster pistols, simple weapons).

Tchaw Fenn

Fenn is a pudgy Bothan of middle years with an impeccable pointed beard, which he often preens in very public places. He refers to himself as a broker. His area of specialization is the same as that of most of his species: information.

For a time, toward the end of Riboga's time in the system, Fenn worked exclusively for the Hutt. Now he's content with brokering information for whatever parties are able to produce sufficient credits. To Fenn, work is work, and he's not going to turn it down when it comes so naturally. He revels in the process of gathering information.

Tchaw Fenn: Male Bothan Scoundrel 3; Init +0; Defense 15 (+5 class); Spd 10 m; WP 12; Atk +2 ranged (3d6, blaster pistol); SQ Illicit barter, better lucky than good; SV Fort +2, Ref +3, Will +3; SZ M; Rep 0; Str 9, Dex 11, Con 12, Int 14, Wis 10, Cha 11.

Skills: Appraise +6, Bluff +6, Computer Use +7, Diplomacy +1, Escape Artist +3, Forgery +5, Gather Information +5, Hide +4, Knowledge (streetwise—Cularin) +7, Listen +5, Pilot +2, Profession (broker) +4, Sleight of Hand +4, Spot +5; Read/Write Bothuese, Speak Basic, Speath Bothuese.

Feats: Iron Will, Low Profile, Weapon Group Proficiencies (blaster pistols, simple weapons).

Hid Toqema

In the interest of appeasing the "cultural unity" movement of their homeworld, the Daedala family hired a group of nearly one hundred Twi'lek engineers to operate the gas mines on Friz Harammel. Hid Toqema, a gray-skinned Twi'lek of advancing years, was one of the first Twi'leks hired.

Hid worked for many years in the design of thermal gas registers, manipulating the microscopic world at a molecular level. As he grew older, however, his reflexes slowed. Many of his coworkers began to take his slow responses as a lack of memory, rather than a sign of the careful consideration they actually represented. Now employed as a "maintenance supervisor" for the third sublevel of the gas mines, Hid shows up for work every day. He loves his job, since it allows him to work at whatever pace he finds comfortable without having to listen to anyone else grouse about getting things done. However, he's always felt himself to be management material and keeps wondering when he'll be promoted.

Hid Toqema: Male Twi'lek Expert 5; Init –1; Defense 10 (+1 class, –1 Dex); Spd 10 m; WP 12; Atk +3 melee and ranged; SQ Low-light vision; SV Fort +1, Ref +0, Will +4; SZ M; Rep 1; Str 11, Dex 9, Con 11, Int 16, Wis 13, Cha 14.

Skills: Computer Use +12, Craft (mining) +7, Gather Information +6, Knowledge (Cularin system) +8, Knowledge (engineering) +11, Knowledge (physical sciences—physics) +9, Profession (janitor) +4, Repair +7; Read/Write Basic, Read/Write Ryu, Speak Basic, Speak Lekku, Speak Ryu.

Feats: Cautious, Gearhead, Weapon Group Proficiency (simple weapons).

Ipsus

Naescorcom is an industrial group from the Outer Rim. Technically a manufacturing consortium, it is controlled by representatives from seven Outer Rim planets, each of which manufactures something slightly different. Five years ago, two of the worlds with representatives in Naescorcom called for a vote on establishing a manufacturing center in Genarius. The location, they argued, should allow easy distribution of their goods to both the Core Worlds and the Outer Rim, with direct access to many of the Mid Rim systems.

While the other representatives agreed the idea had some initial merit, they could not bring themselves to commit the full resources of Naescorcom to the project. They provided a startup budget of only 50 million credits, noting that the initial recuperation of those funds would be the responsibility of the two worlds that requested the city. Construction on Ipsus began soon thereafter. The design of the city was purely functional, with almost no attempt at decoration or ornamentation. The boxlike buildings stood in long rows with narrow walkways connecting them. Seven sections were completed, but five still stand empty, since Ipsus has not yet hit the break-even point. The other two are busy putting their wares into circulation.

Line One is a series of buildings where textiles are manufactured. While the market for textiles is not enormous in any section of the galaxy, they remain one of those minor necessities that provide a steady (if unexciting) form of income. Very little security is put on these buildings, simply because Naescorcom has a hard time believing anyone would want to steal their textiles.

Line Two is a sharp contrast. Patrolled by heavily armed Naescorcom guards, the buildings of Line Two have double-reinforced blast doors at the main entrance. All of the work gets done far below the city proper. When the difficult aspects of the production process have been completed, Naescorcom's thermal detonators are gently loaded into crates for shipment.

Diversification, Naescorcom argues, is the key to success in the modern galaxy. While textiles and thermal detonators may seem like extreme examples of diversification within a single consortium, the other Naescorcom member worlds offer even stranger combinations of goods. If all goes well, those products will soon be represented in the Cularin system as well.

Ipsus is governed remotely by the Naescorcom board. Locally, two operations overseers ensure that the lines are moving properly.

Loa Tibeeme

One of the problems Naescorcom had in its early years was network security. Outer Rim technologies had trouble keeping pace with criminals from the Core Worlds. As a result, while Naescorcom developed numerous new tools and programs, slicers from other systems typically stole their data from other systems before Naescorcom could put them into the marketplace. A single slicer was eventually tracked down, a young Rodian named Loa Tibeeme who had left enough electronic suckerprints all over the Naescorcom network that no amount of legal maneuvering could help him.

Rather than turning her over to the authorities, the corporation decided that Loa's abilities might come in handy. She thus became something of an indentured servant, working off her transgression against Naescorcom. She will have her revenge, however. Quiet and given to plotting, she has built backdoors into every Naescorcom system she's worked on.

She's currently on Ipsus, advising other programmers on setting up proper security measures and trying to decide if there is likely to be any information she might need access to some day.

Loa Tibeeme: Female Rodian Expert 6; Init +1; Defense 13 (+2 class, +1 Dex); Spd 10 m; WP 11; Atk +4 ranged (3d6, blaster pistol); SQ +2 species bonus to Search, Spot, and Listen checks; SV Fort +2, Ref +3, Will +6; SZ M; Rep 1; Str 10, Dex 13, Con 11, Int 14, Wis 12, Cha 10.

 Skills: Computer Use +16, Craft (electronics) +12, Knowledge (streetwise—Cularin) +8, Repair +8, Survival +4; Read/Write Rodese, Read/Write Basic, Speak Basic, Speak Rodese, Speak Huttese, Speak Tarasinese.

 Feats: Gearhead, Skill Emphasis (Computer Use), Skill Emphasis (Craft [electronics]), Track, Weapon Group Proficiency (simple weapons).

Nui Gneppe

Gneppe is a thin-faced Filordi who walks with one shoulder several inches higher than the other. He is the archivist for Line Two. He records all activities undertaken by Line Two, particularly anything that results in an explosion. Naescorcom monitors the destruction of property very closely. Current thinking is that the benefits of being one of the few legitimate manufacturers of thermal detonators in

this sector are worth the risk. So far, this thinking has not been shown inaccurate.

 Gneppe entered the employ of Naescorcom after getting bored with the activities of the Trade Federation, for whom he worked more than a decade. He loves telling stories about the feuds between the Cartel and the Trade Federation. He does a hilariously accurate impression of a frightened Neimoidian calling for droideka support. In his spare time, Gneppe reads history text files.

Nui Gneppe: Male Filordi Expert 4; Init +2; Defense 13 (+1 class, +2 Dex); Spd 14m; WP 11; Atk +4 melee (1d6, 2 pincers), +5 ranged (3d6, blaster pistol); SQ +4 species bonus to Listen checks; SV Fort +1, Ref +3, Will +4; SZ M; Rep 0; Str 12, Dex 14, Con 11, Int 13, Wis 11, Cha 10.

 Skills: Computer Use +5, Knowledge (bureaucracy) +6, Knowledge (galactic history) +10, Listen +2, Profession (archivist) +7; Read/Write Filordis, Speak Basic, Speak Filordis.

 Feats: Sharp-Eyed, Skill Emphasis (Knowledge [galactic history]), Weapon Group Proficiency (simple weapons).

Tolea Biqua

From a distance, Tolea Biqua looks like a brilliant, multi-colored painting set into the swirling colors of the clouds of Genarius. It conjures images of beautiful sunsets, viewed through a prism the size of the sky. It has drawn the attention of many travelers, much to their dismay. It is only when the observer gets close enough to make out details that the garish mishmash of colors and shapes becomes apparent. Far from beautiful, Tolea Biqua looks disorganized and disheveled. It is as though every leftover piece of every floating city ever created had been put into a bag, shaken, and dumped out to form a huge city encompassing everything.

 Tolea Biqua is thus, in many respects, a monument to bad taste and excess. Built on Riboga's command, the city reflects everything the "Exalted Disgusting One" wanted. (The common folk of Tolea Biqua once used this title used to refer to Riboga. This made him laugh the first time he heard it. The second time, he demanded a higher share of profits from every business in the city.) Buildings were constructed at irregular intervals, facing in all directions. No uniform shape was chosen for the buildings, either. Hemispheres sit beside boxlike warehouses, which sit beside towers, which overlook cones flanked by pyramids. Every surface has been painted with glowing paints, and the edge of every rooftop is lined with bright red, green, or purple neon tubes.

 Almost any vice can be accommodated in Tolea Biqua (or Varna Biqua), although the most profitable industry by far is gambling. Multiple gambling establishments operate simultaneously on Tolea Biqua, but the most profitable by far is Riboga's Barge, a gambling hall converted from the floating barge Riboga left behind when he lost control of the Cularin smugglers to Nirama. Had he known who was going to buy

it, Riboga might have been somewhat more cautious in his sales, but at the time he didn't care.

The two Trandoshans who bought the barge have a long-standing history of bad blood with Hutts, so the opportunity to own a Hutt's sail barge was too much to pass up. They built two distinct sections into the barge, a public area accessible to anyone who could pay the modest cover fee (50 credits) and a members' section. There, the high stakes games took place, and patrons could lounge in the type of comfort normally afforded only to Hutts. The Trandoshans even converted Riboga's bathing pool into an enormous hot tub large enough for twenty Humans at a time. They even turned the never-used breeding chamber into a "Museum of Useless Inventions," a none too subtle jab at Riboga's virility (or lack thereof).

An interesting factoid about Tolea Biqua is that the number of bars is higher than the number of all other businesses (legitimate or otherwise) combined. Bars range from horrid dives to very refined, upper crust locales where drinks are sniffed and sipped, rather than slugged and spat. There is no geographic delineation of where the "good" and "bad" bars are. Nor is there any way to tell from the name of the bar which category is the most appropriate. It takes the typical visitor to Tolea Biqua about five bars and three fights to find the right place to drink.

Tolea Biqua's niche revolves around public vices. Gambling, drinking, companionship, glitterstim—these are all available within the wondrous glowing city of Tolea Biqua. Nothing that goes on inside Tolea Biqua is ever discussed outside, except in the most general terms. This anonymity, as much as anything, is what keeps Tolea Biqua prosperous.

Lalo

A Twi'lek trained in the art of massage, Lalo is rarely hired directly by her clients. She's sent as a "gift" for them instead. She only performs massage, nothing more, but her massages typically leave even the most problematic customers virtually unconscious by the time she's done. Sometimes she leaves clients fully unconscious, and when she's paid enough, she's willing to practice a needle-based massage therapy. Unfortunately, those needles frequently slip as she uses them, managing to find their way into a vital organ. Lalo is good at what she does, both massage and assassination. She honed her skills under one of Riboga's commandants, but fortunately, Riboga killed that assistant instead of returning to Nal Hutta with him.

Lalo: Female Twi'lek Scoundrel 5; Init +2; Defense 18 (+6 class, +2 Dex); Spd 10 m; WP 15/10; Atk +6 melee (1, needle), +1 ranged (3d4, hold-out blaster); SA Better lucky than good, Skill Emphasis (Profession), sneak attack +2d6; SQ Low-light vision; SV Fort +1, Ref +6, Will +2; SZ M; Rep 3; Str 11, Dex 15, Con 10, Int 13, Wis 12, Cha 17.

Skills: Hide +10, Intimidate +11, Knowledge (life sciences—anatomy) +9, Knowledge (streetwise—Cularin) +9, Listen +9, Move Silently +10, Profession (masseuse) +13, Sleight of Hand +10, Spot +9; Read/Write Basic, Read/Write Ryu, Speak Basic, Speak Lekku, Speak Ryu, Speak Huttese.

Feats: Force-Sensitive, Weapon Focus (needle), Weapon Finesse (needle), Weapon Group Proficiency (simple weapons).

Bez

Bez is a Human dealer located in the "cheap" area of Riboga's Barge. He is a middle-aged Human with close-cropped blonde hair and a scar that runs all the way across his fore-head. His nose is crooked, looking like it's been broken, set, and rebroken a number of times. His hands look more like thick-knuckled paws. Before becoming a dealer at the casino, Bez served drinks on the original barge, when Riboga himself was in charge. His scars are the result of Riboga repeatedly sending his favorite waiter into single combat with various other creatures from around the galaxy. Bez always won, and even understood why the Hutt did what he did, but he shed no tears when the Hutt went home.

Bez: Male Human Thug 9; Init +1; Defense 14 (+3 class, +1 Dex); Spd 10 m; WP 15; Atk +11/+6 melee (2d6, vibroblade), +10/+5 ranged; SV Fort +7, Ref +4, Will +4; SZ M; Rep 2; Str 15, Dex 13, Con 12, Int 11, Wis 12, Cha 9.

Skills: Profession (bartender) +10, Intimidate +7, Knowledge (streetwise—Cularin) +9, Listen +4, Spot +4; Read/Write Basic, Speak Basic.

Feats: Armor Proficiency (light), Dodge, Toughness, Weapon Focus (vibroblade), Weapon Group Proficiencies (simple weapons, vibro weapons).

Varna Biqua

Varna Biqua sports more vice and less fanfare than her sister city Tolea Biqua. Shrouded in a particularly thick cloud bank, Varna Biqua is a centerpoint for illicit trade. (Some speculate that the cloud bank was enhanced by Riboga to hide something, although this was never proven.) While the Smugglers' Confederation doesn't pay much attention to Varna Biqua anymore, the pirates of the system certainly do. Those who have been to Varna Biqua speak of a lot of recent building, focusing on a new docking bay. From what they've said, the bay might be able to accommodate a Republic cruiser.

Illegal substances and weapons are two of the commodities traded most frequently in Varna Biqua. The black market there is extensive. Almost anything is available for a price. The city is every bit as chaotic as Tolea Biqua is excessive. The motto on Varna Biqua is: "Live and let live . . . unless they get in your way. Then kill them." This vigilante attitude leads to numerous tussles and more than a few murders, but there aren't many on Varna Biqua who care. Visitors to the city are given every opportunity to reconsider before stepping foot off their ship. Once they leave the safety of their transport, they're on their own.

30

Piknab Carsels

At an early age, Piknab Carsels left Naboo to seek fame and fortune. He never returned to Otoh Gunga. Instead, the Gungan enrolled in one flight school after another, picking up tips about how to fly every kind of ship in existence. His favorites were always starfighters. Shortly before his twenty-sixth birthday, Piknab made the leap and purchased his own starfighter, arranging financing through Riboga and the Smugglers' Confederation. He developed quite a reputation as an ace pilot, but unfortunately for him, reputation doesn't pay bills. He ended up delinquent on several payments in a row, so Riboga the Hutt sent a trio of collection agents to take care of Piknab, starting with his big floppy ears.

When the thugs made their first incisions, Piknab surrendered and asked to be given another option. Ever since, he's been working off his debt to Riboga. Although the Hutt has left the system, Piknab remains in place, still doing everything he did before Riboga lost the system to Nirama.

Piknab Carsels: Male Gungan Fringer 8/Starfighter Ace 4; Init +3; Defense 21 (+8 class, +3 Dex); Spd 10 m; VP/WP 52/11; Atk +13/+8 ranged (3d6, blaster pistol); SA Barter, adaptive learning (Astrogate, Repair), jury-rig +4, survival, starfighter defense +4, familiarity +2 (his ship, the *Gungan Glory*); SQ Low-light vision, hold breath; SV Fort +8, Ref +11, Will +4; SZ M; Rep 3; Str 11, Dex 16, Con 11, Int 14, Wis 10, Cha 11.

Skills : Astrogate +15, Computer Use +11, Pilot +20, Repair +11, Hide +6, Knowledge (Naboo system) +3, Knowledge (Cularin system) +9, Knowledge (streetwise–Cularin) +9, Listen +2, Spot +12, Survival +8, Swim +10; Read/Write Basic, Speak Basic, Speak Huttese.

Feats: Gearhead, Run, Spacer, Starfighter Dodge, Starfighter Operation (starfighter), Weapon Group Proficiencies (blaster pistols, simple weapons, starship weapons).

Quaad Endac

Quaad Endac is one of those individuals who can obtain anything, and as such, is one of the prime movers in Varna Biqua. He is somewhat enigmatic, though, only showing up when he knows a great deal of money or potential amusement is involved. When he appears, he is typically in disguise. Sometimes he's an old crone, sometimes he's a balding man of later years, and sometimes he's a younger man. Once, he went through a rigorous makeup routine to look like a Cerean. No one knows exactly what Quaad really looks like. He typically identifies himself by wearing a cutting from a ny'yosin bush, a plant native to Cularin.

In dealing with others, Quaad is very businesslike. He never cracks jokes, and he looks askance at anyone who dares to do so in his presence. Business is business. If they wanted to laugh, they should have taken in a show.

Quaad Endac: Male Human Expert 12; Init +5; Defense 15 (+4 class, +1 Dex); Spd 10 m; WP 12; Atk +10/+5 ranged (3d6, blaster pistol); SV Fort +5, Ref +5, Will +10; SZ M; Rep 5; Str 12, Dex 13, Con 12, Int 13, Wis 14, Cha 15.

Skills: Computer Use +12, Disable Device +3, Disguise +19, Entertain (acting) +8, Hide +10, Knowledge (business–scavenging) +14, Knowledge (streetwise–Cularin) +14, Listen +10, Profession (smuggler) +14, Search +7, Spot +10; Read/Write Basic, Speak Basic.

Feats: Alertness, Improved Initiative, Mimic, Skill Emphasis (Disguise), Stealthy, Weapon Group Proficiencies (blaster pistols, simple weapons).

Ulbasca

> ### Ulbasca at a Glance
> **Type:** Rocky moon
> **Climate:** Cold rocky desert
> **Length of Day:** Eternal
> **Length of Year:** 1,424 standard days

Ulbasca's terrain is flat and rocky, with little vegetation at all. The atmosphere contains enough oxygen to support a variety of lifeforms, including Humans, but it also contains traces of gases poisonous to most of the races in the known galaxy. Breath masks are required if a being wants to spend more than a couple of hours on the surface. Small mountains and rocky canyons break the monotonous flatness of most of the surface. These canyons support the few lifeforms native to this place.

The strangest feature of this moon is its orbit around Genarius. Ulbasca marks a path through the heavens that keeps it constantly in the light of Cularin's suns. Because the dark side is bathed by light from Genarius itself, it is never truly night there at all. The darkest time is a short twilight period when one side faces away from the suns; this lasts for about nine hours.

Small reptiles existing on sulfurous plants rule this world. Indeed, they are the only form of animal life. The lizards come in various sizes and fill all ecological niches. Some of the larger ones prey on the smaller ones. These reptiles are, for the most part, like the snakes of other worlds. Some have short legs they use while climbing the rocky canyons. Larger snakes can be as long as 40 meters and can swallow a Human whole.

The moon's mineral survey indicated a collection of the most common elements in the galaxy, with nothing of any real value. Thus, there has been no attempt to land a colony there when the other habitable planets offer more interesting places to live. Despite the lack of reasons to claim the moon, the leaders of Ipsus and Edic Bar both claim ownership. Both companies, SoroSuub Corporation and Naescorcom, show no more interest in exploiting the moon than anyone else, but occasionally argue over mining rights. Both corporations

have landed survey expeditions, and both have claimed the moon as their own. No one is really sure why.

Ostfrei

Ostfrei at a Glance
Type: Rocky moon
Climate: Cold rocky wasteland
Length of Day: 27 standard hours
Length of Year: 1,424 standard days

A dark moon, Ostfrei is the counterpart to Ulbasca in the orbital scheme of Genarius. Whereas Ulbasca is always light, Ostfrei is nearly always dark. Its orbit is such that Genarius sits between it and the suns for all but two hours of its day, and the light from Genarius barely penetrates to the surface. The atmosphere is composed of carbon monoxide and methane, with soot particles floating like great clouds. The gases refract the incoming light so that very little of it can reach the surface at all. The moon is not habitable, and no natural lifeforms occur.

The moon itself is another rocky accumulation of the most common elements known. Like Ulbasca, it generates no interest among the corporations in the system. It is just not worth the expense of erecting sealed environments to extract minerals that are more easily available elsewhere. The surface is a twisted network of channels, crevasses, and ridges. A few volcanoes, spaced far apart, spew soot and dust into the air, but rarely erupt with lava flows. The core of the moon is theorized to be too cold for sustained eruptions. In the past, this moon was habitable and bore a close resemblance to Ulbasca. It was, however, too close to the explosion that produced the asteroid belt. A few asteroids rained down on Ostfrei when the former planet broke apart. The asteroids started a chain of events that turned the moon into the wasteland it is today.

The only activity of note around the moon in recent times has been the presence of Republic cruisers in orbit. Residents of Genarius have speculated idly about what Colonel Tramsig might be doing, but no one really cares enough to investigate. The cruisers come and go, and they don't stay long. Sometimes they exchange troops or supplies. No one ever sees shuttles descend to the moon's surface.

Uffel

Uffel at a Glance
Type: Uninhabitable moon
Climate: Poisonous to living beings
Length of Day: 19 standard hours
Length of Year: 1,424 standard days

The moon of Uffel supports a thick atmosphere filled with numerous heavy and poisonous gases. The small moon

rotates quickly around Genarius, spending equal time in light and darkness. Because of the faint light emitted by Genarius itself, it would never really be dark on the moon if it were not for the atmosphere. Thick gases dim the light as it travels toward the planet's surface, with the result that it is usually twilight or night. Days are never as bright as they are on Cularin or Genarius.

Though uninhabitable, the moon's potential mineral wealth was attractive enough to two Twi'leks that they mounted a survey expedition. When their ship hit the thick atmosphere, they lost control. The ship was pummeled, twisted, and broken, and the winds cast the pieces to the surface. The Twi'leks did not survive, but three droids emerged from the wreckage more or less functional. Two were astromech droids of the R4 series. The third was QS-2D, a heavily modified humanoid administrative droid based on a protocol droid frame. 2D surveyed the situation and decided that because its owner was dead, it was independent.

Over the next few days, 2D and the R4 units repaired themselves, affixed some makeshift environmental protection, and assessed the ship's circuitry for working components. During these repairs, 2D programmed the astromech droids to know it as their master. Finding the comlink and some other sensory equipment operational, the droids surveyed the nearby landscape and decided that their ship would make a good settlement location.

With the comlink repaired, 2D directed his two astromechs, R4-S2 and R4-J9, to survey mineral deposits for mining purposes. The results showed a promising vein of valuable ore near the ship's site, and 2D contacted Riboga the Hutt. Acting in the name of its dead master, 2D made a deal with Riboga to acquire additional droids in exchange for a share of the profits of the mining operations. Soon power droids, miner droids, more astromechs, and even a protocol droid arrived. All of these were reprogrammed to acknowledge QS-2D as their master. Facilities were built, and the mines started to turn a profit. The profits were reinvested in more equipment, including a droid manufacturing facility. Within a few years, a hundred or more droids called the moon home, all "owned" by 2D.

When the mines began to run dry, 2D was prepared. It had been exploring new droid designs and manufactured a prototype MSF droid, a variant on the MSE "mouse droid," that could perform minor mechanical repairs and carry messages. Furthermore, it could hover on tiny repulsorlift engines and work in extremely cramped conditions. The prototype was well received. The profits from the droid manufacture allowed 2D to buy Riboga's interest in the mines just before the crimelord lost the system to Nirama.

Uffel Today

Under the camouflage of the red-brown atmosphere, Uffel has seen quite a transformation. QS-2D has bought, constructed, or in some cases, stolen a great many droids. It now has more than a thousand of them. They all work industriously and enjoy their "freedom" from the control of living beings. QS-2D maintains strict control over their routines, but their responsibilities are logical and predictable. The original mines no longer produce, but worker droids plunder new mines. The settlement around the crashed ship has been abandoned. A larger city called X2-4 houses the droids and their facilities. It sells some of the minerals and uses the rest to create new droids. Some droids from the factory join the colony, while others are sold offworld. A spaceport has been built in X2-4 that functions as perhaps the largest droid ever created: the whole space station is controlled by a single droid with multiple coprocessors.

QS-2D's greatest creation, an engineering droid named G-8Y5, develops new droids, makes modifications to existing droid models, and keeps the droids in the colony functioning. The popularity of the MSF series resulted in a large influx of credits, many of which were spent to update the droid design and construction facilities. Now it is not unusual to see someone on Genarius with a strange-looking droid the owner claims is a prototype from Uffel. Some of them even are.

The droid construction facility is the center of X2-4, but other operations take place there too. The droids work constantly, but without the desire for wealth, they use the results of their labor to enlarge or improve their city. Under

2D's leadership, a huge amount of wealth goes into maintaining everything in X2-4 at peak condition.

Defense is always a primary concern with QS-2D, because it would be easy for a predatory species to come in and assume control of the whole settlement. The droid facility has produced a highly skilled war droid to defend their base of operations. G-8Y5 has designed and built several droid-based space defense weapons platforms. The atmosphere itself aids in the defense. The pilot who can bring a ship down without droid aid is rare indeed. The defenses were tested just a year before the Trade Federation was driven from the system. Four pirate craft broke through the atmosphere and tried to make a landing. One survived the heavy fire from the droid turbo-laser batteries. The crew of the surviving ship met its fate at the hands of the war droid defenders.

Living beings rarely come here, but they do come. QS-2D holds meetings with clients, buyers come to examine the droid facilities and test out new models, and wealthy people come to commission modifications to their own droids. Breath masks and pressure suits are required, because the droids do not build environmental controls into their structures. Near the spaceport a visitor can find accommodations suitable for living beings. Except during inspection tours, the spaceport is usually the only place one finds living beings on the moon. 2D believes that this increases the moon's security.

QS-2D is one of the more powerful corporate movers in the system, but it keeps the lowest profile. It still conducts business in the name of its dead master, so no one can really verify that the poor Twi'lek is dead. The construction facilities produce droids that are used all over the system, some of which carry secret espionage programming as well. Nirama is the only one who refuses to use any of X2-4's products in his operations.

QS-2D

Some previous owner took this basic protocol droid frame and modified it heavily. It now supports a weapons mount for a blaster pistol where its left hand was. Deep black plating acts as armor against blaster fire. Its basic function was replaced with administrative capabilities. QS-2D became a combination personal assistant and bodyguard rather than a translator. The addition of a heuristic processor made 2D capable of long-term independent functions. After some years of duties that required it to act on its own, it developed into an independent droid. When its latest master died, the choice of permanent independent operation was a natural one.

QS-2D is practical yet demanding, always requiring perfection when possible, but willing to adapt to less perfect conditions when necessary. It has a gift for administration beyond its programming and has developed a creative streak. The droid is not trusting of living beings anymore, seeing itself as a possible victim in every encounter. It is prone to become impatient with living beings that hold back information, delay, or are slow to give needed information.

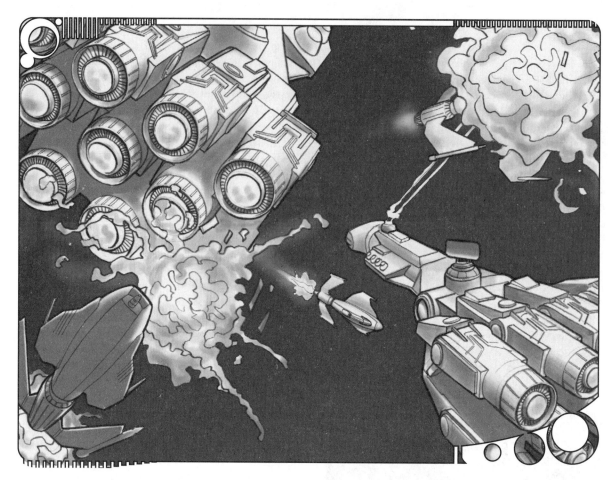

QS-2D: Walking protocol/security droid Expert 7; Init +0; Defense 15 (+5 armor); Spd 8 m; WP 11; Atk +5 ranged (3d6, blaster pistol); SV Fort +2, Ref +2, Will +6; SZ M; Rep 4; Str 10, Dex 11, Con 11, Int 15, Wis 13, Cha 10.

Equipment: Vocabulator, heuristic processor, weapons mount, blaster pistol, environmental compensator, internal hidden comlink, improved sensor package, armor (light).

Skills: Computer Use +9, Craft (electronics–droids) +7, Knowledge (bureaucracy) +9, Knowledge (business) +12, Knowledge (Cularin–flora) +5, Repair +9, Search +7, Spot +6, Survival +6; Speak Basic.

Feats: Armor Proficiency (light), Skill Emphasis (Knowledge [business]), Weapon Group Proficiency (blaster pistols).

R4-S2

R4-S2 was a maintenance droid on board the original Twi'lek ship. It was responsible for keeping the electronic systems functioning properly and making minor repairs. Small for an astromech droid, it sports a mushroom-shaped head on a telescopic "neck" designed to allow it visual access to higher sections of the ship. Its color scheme is red and gold.

R4-S2: Tracked astromech droid Expert 4; Init +2; Defense 14 (+1 class, +2 Dex, +1 size); Spd 8 m; WP 14; Atk +5 melee and ranged (no weapons); SV Fort +3, Ref +3, Will +5; SZ S; Rep 0; Str 14, Dex 14, Con 14, Int 16, Wis 12, Cha 11.

Equipment: Heuristic processor, environmental compensator, diagnostics package, improved sensor package, infrared vision, tool mounts (×5), telescopic appendage (×3), magnetic feet, fire extinguisher.

Skills: Astrogate +8, Computer Use +8, Craft (mechanics) +8, Disable Device +8, Pilot +7, Repair +11, Spot +5; Speak Basic.

Feats: Cautious, Skill Emphasis (Repair).

4-KT

4-KT is a thin humanoid droid that closely resembles a silver skeleton. It has bright yellow eyes set into deep sockets. Its head is slightly oblong, sporting an extra boxlike appendage at the rear. Its arms end in hands with ten long fingers each. The extra fingers are typically held together outstretched when they're not actively working. When they are working, they deftly manipulate items with amazing precision.

Originally trained as a medical droid, 4-KT was one of the first droids acquired by QS-2D. It was eventually reprogrammed for droid development. 4-KT works relentlessly, completely draining its power cells on occasion. It enjoys the creative work of droid design, working very well with G-8Y5.

4-KT: Walking medical droid Expert 3; Init +4; Defense 15 (+1 class, +4 Dex); Spd 8 m; WP 13; Atk +3 melee, +6 ranged (no weapons); SV Fort +2, Ref +5, Will +2; SZ M; Rep 0; Str 12, Dex 18, Con 13, Int 16, Wis 9, Cha 11.

Equipment: Environmental compensator, extra fingers on each hand, vocabulator, recording unit (video and audio), locked access.

Skills: Computer Use +8, Craft (engineering—droids) + 11, Knowledge (physical sciences—physics) +8, Repair +11, Spot +2, Search +5; Speak Basic.

Feats: Skill Emphasis (Craft [engineering—droids]), Skill Emphasis (Repair).

HG-211

Head of security for the droid construction facilities, HG-211 is a tightly programmed enforcer. Its gunmetal gray torso is crisscrossed with thick black stripes. A thin red wire has been stretched across one of the stripes as a very visible self-destruct mechanism. Only 211 knows how to activate it, but will not hesitate to do so in defense of the colony.

HG-211: Walking security droid Thug 9; Init +2; Defense 16 (+2 Dex, +4 armor); Spd 8 m; WP 15; Atk +11/+6 ranged with one pistol, +9/+9/+6 ranged with two pistols (3d8, heavy blaster pistol); SV Fort +5, Ref +5, Will +7; SZ M; Rep 0; Str 16, Dex 14, Con 15, Int 13, Wis 12, Cha 10.

Equipment: Environmental compensator, weapons mount (×2), improved sensor package, motion detectors, infrared vision, self-destruct mechanism, locked access.

Skills: Listen +10, Profession (security guard) +11, Search +10, Spot +11, Survival +8; Understand Basic.

Feats: Ambidexterity, Armor Proficiency (light), Point Blank Shot, Two-Weapon Fighting, Weapon Group Proficiencies (simple weapons, blaster pistols).

MSF-F2

The original prototype of the popular MSF line, MSF-F2 is the only newly configured mouse droid QS-2D kept. The tiny box-shaped droid will follow any nondroids visiting X2-4. Its silver-trimmed body almost waddles, due to an uneven calibration it has developed in its wheel wells over the years. F2 follows outsiders so that QS-2D knows where they are. The little droid is quite open about this practice, and as such, visitors usually tolerate it. Some have tried to evade him, but the little droid somehow seems to be everywhere at once.

MSF-F2: Wheeled message droid Expert 1; Init +4; Defense 16 (+4 Dex, +2 size); Spd 12m; WP 10; Atk −1 melee, +4 ranged (no weapons); SV Fort −1, Ref +4, Will +2; SZ T; Rep 0; Str 8, Dex 18, Con 10, Int 12, Wis 10, Cha 10.

Equipment: Environmental compensator, recording unit (video and audio), tool mount (×2), small telescopic arms (×2), internal comlink, locked access.

Skills: Listen +2, Repair +3, Search +3, Spot +2.

Feats: Sharp-Eyed.

Eskaron

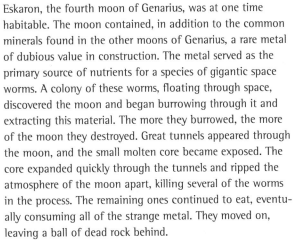

Eskaron at a Glance

Type: Perforated rocky moon
Climate: None
Length of Day: 20 standard hours
Length of Year: 1,424 standard days

Eskaron, the fourth moon of Genarius, was at one time habitable. The moon contained, in addition to the common minerals found in the other moons of Genarius, a rare metal of dubious value in construction. The metal served as the primary source of nutrients for a species of gigantic space worms. A colony of these worms, floating through space, discovered the moon and began burrowing through it and extracting this material. The more they burrowed, the more of the moon they destroyed. Great tunnels appeared through the moon, and the small molten core became exposed. The core expanded quickly through the tunnels and ripped the atmosphere of the moon apart, killing several of the worms in the process. The remaining ones continued to eat, eventually consuming all of the strange metal. They moved on, leaving a ball of dead rock behind.

The moon retained the tunnels, some several kilometers wide and some only a few meters wide. The tunnels run through the diameter of the moon, crisscrossing and connecting many times. The tunnels have created value in the moon, which would otherwise be left completely alone. Riboga the Hutt began sponsoring starfighter races through the tunnels some 40 standard years ago. Nirama has continued the tradition. Teams have formed to compete in these races, and the sport has caught on. It is now a common sight to see several space yachts in orbit around Eskaron. Visitors watch the races or observe practice sessions. Nirama takes a cut of most of the race revenue and bets heavily on the racers. While not officially owning the moon, Nirama maintains control of the activity there. No one questions his right to do so.

The moon is also used by reckless adventurers testing their piloting skills, and by those who seek to challenge each other over matters of honor. One gang of young toughs, the Blood Velkers, has even taken to racing the tunnels as a rite of initiation. Members of the Velkers can be found on Tolea Biqua and Varna Biqua, causing trouble and amusing themselves at the expense of honest residents.

Asteroid Belt

The Belt at a Glance

Type: Asteroid belt
Climate: None
Length of Day: Not applicable
Length of Year: 3,924 standard days

Where the asteroid belt is now, a lush jungle planet once orbited the suns of Cularin. Internal stresses caused a cataclysmic chain reaction, resulting in the breakup of the planet itself. The resultant asteroids settled into the former planet's orbit, stretching out around the orbital path. Few escaped. The asteroid belt is very thin, but most of the asteroids are only a few kilometers across. The core of the planet formed the largest asteroid, some 400 kilometers across. The asteroids themselves have irregular orbits within the belt, but few asteroids ever escape the belt entirely.

The asteroids are home to two separate predatory groups. Nirama's criminal organization owns the largest asteroid, while his smugglers work from several smaller bases among the floating rocks. Farther away from Riboga's old stronghold, pirate fleets hide behind some of the larger asteroids. The pirates change base locations frequently to avoid detection by Nirama and the military, but the smaller smuggler bases are protected by the crimelord.

The asteroid belt makes a perfect place to attack incoming freighters. Most ships have to stop at the belt, then either fly through it at sublight speeds or go around. Pirates seem well informed about where and when this might happen. Their ships converge on freighters as soon as they emerge from hyperspace, pick them dry, and then disappear into the relative safety of the rocks. These attacks happen so rapidly that the military has little or no time to respond. To counter the rapid attacks, Colonel Tramsig recently laid a trap by sending military cruisers instead of freighters on several trips. In a surprising ambush, one cruiser destroyed five pirate vessels. The pirates have since become more cautious in their attacks.

Other than criminals, the asteroid belt boasts only one resident, a man named Xav Verivax. Xav is known for mixing with the cream of society and for doing outrageous and unexpected things. Even his friends don't understand him.

Xav Verivax

Xav, a former member of the Republic army, is now a playboy freighter captain. He makes short runs within the system whenever he feels like doing so. He seems always to have enough credits and claims to live in the asteroid belt simply to have some privacy. He is frequently seen on Cularin in the platform cities, or in Tolea Biqua on Genarius. As an elite slacker, he treats those around him with a playful superiority, as if he is amusedly tolerating them. This attitude can be annoying, but no one has successfully challenged Xav and lived, so people put up with him.

Tall, with fair hair and well-tanned skin, Xav is handsome and carries himself with a debonair surety. Nothing ever seems to surprise or upset him. His eyes can twinkle knowingly when he makes a jest, or show his contempt for someone trying too hard to please him. When forced into combat, he becomes ruthlessly efficient, but as soon as his foes are dead, he resumes his jaunty attitude.

Xav Verivax: Male Human Soldier 8/Noble 4; Init +3; Defense 18 (+3 Dex, +5 combat jumpsuit); Spd 10 m;

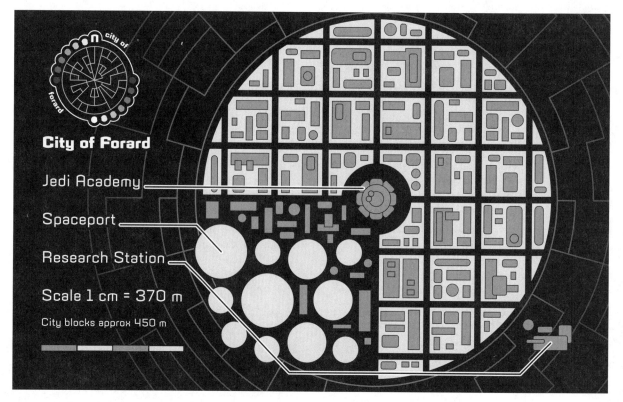

City of Forard

Jedi Academy

Spaceport

Research Station

Scale 1 cm = 370 m

City blocks approx 450 m

VP/WP 108/16; Atk +13/+8/+3 melee (2d6+2, vibroblade), +14/+9/+4 ranged *or* +8/+8/+8/+8/+3/–2 ranged (3d8, heavy blaster pistol); SA Call in a favor, inspire confidence, command; SV Fort +6, Ref +11, Will +10; SZ M; FP 10; Rep 9; Str 15, Dex 17, Con 16, Int 15, Wis 14, Cha 15.

Equipment: Two heavy blaster pistols, combat jumpsuit.

Skills: Astrogate +11, Bluff +7, Computer Use +11, Demolitions +9, Diplomacy +6, Knowledge (culture–military) +9, Knowledge (Cularin system) +11, Knowledge (spacer lore) +7, Knowledge (galactic politics) +8, Pilot +15, Search +8, Sense Motive +8, Spot +4; Read/Write Basic, Speak Basic, Speak Tarasinese.

Feats: Ambidexterity, Armor Proficiencies (light, medium, heavy), Multishot, Point Blank Shot, Quick Draw, Rapid Shot, Skill Emphasis (Bluff), Spacer, Two-Weapon Fighting, Weapon Focus (heavy blaster pistol), Weapon Group Proficiencies (blaster pistols, blaster rifles, heavy weapons, simple weapons, vibro weapons).

Almas

Almas at a Glance

Type: Terraformed terrestrial
Climate: Temperate grasslands, desolate wasteland
Length of Day: 38 standard hours
Length of Year: 8,784 standard days

Orbiting far from the suns of the Cularin system, the small planet of Almas would be unremarkable except for its importance in the history of the Jedi. The planet itself is an anomaly in space: a molten terrestrial planet orbiting beyond the usual range for such planets. The core is hot, but the surface would normally be covered with ice. The planet's original atmosphere contained methane, phosphorus, and other heavy gases, all of them poisonous. That did not deter a Sith Lord named Darth Rivan from choosing the planet as his home. Darth Rivan built a fortress and enclosed the whole structure in a dome.

But Rivan was not content to leave nature to its own devices. Combining his expertise in biolog with the power of the Force, he developed a new species of plant called kaluthin. Kaluthin is a wavy, grasslike plant. Its leaves are green on the edges and deeply purple in the center. The stalks are generally greenish, but also contain white areas that mark phosphorus deposits. Kaluthin's unique properties include the ability to synthesize methane from the air and create oxygen. Its taproots reach miles into the crust of the planet. After Darth Rivan spread kaluthin across the surface of Almas, the plants slowly changed the local environment. The taproots brought heat from the center of the planet, and the methane processing changed the atmosphere. As the plants processed the phosphorus in the air, the mineral accumulated in the plants' structure, and they began to glow. Before he was slain, his creations had

begun to terraform the planet from an unlivable nightmare into the gardenlike world it is today.

Darth Rivan was driven from Almas by Jedi during the Sith Wars, and his domelike home was blasted into pieces. The central fortress remained, impervious to blaster fire. The Jedi, thinking that the fortress was not worth the continued effort, decided to leave it. Centuries passed. The kaluthin continued to prosper, spreading across the whole planet. By the time Reidi Artom came to Cularin, the planet supported an oxygen atmosphere a little richer than Humans consider normal. Trace elements of methane and phosphorus make the air slightly poisonous as well, but after a visitor starts breathing the atmosphere, he won't notice adverse health conditions until he's had several months of exposure. Breath masks are strongly recommended.

Though the planet is far from the suns, and therefore receives little light, the surface is always illuminated by Cularin's moonlight. Leaves of kaluthin, glowing with phosphorus, are responsible. It can be a little unsettling for visitors to see the light coming from the planet rather than the sky.

Materially, the planet is poorly suited for mining. The expense of establishing a mining operation does not outweigh the value of the small mineral deposits in the planet's crust, and removing the kaluthin would cause the planet's atmosphere to become unstable. Thus, the planet is more like a living plant than anything else; the roots of the kaluthin bind the soil together.

Almas has two mountain ranges, each one about 200 kilometers long. The mountains are far from the settlements, and the fields of kaluthin do not grow all the way to their peaks. Almas has no surface water, but below the surface, there are large underground lakes where the icy crust has melted. The kaluthin all nourish themselves from these underground lakes, and settlers dig deep wells to mine the precious water.

From space, Almas looks like a planet of contrasting, and conflicting, environments. Over much of the surface, the kaluthin grow. Other plants have been introduced into the soil, but only those that survive form a symbiotic relationship with the kaluthin. On the far side of the planet, there is a desolate wasteland where even kaluthin cannot grow anymore. The ancient Sith fortress, now partially buried, is at the center of this wasteland. The "dead zone" surrounding it is slowly expanding. Jedi have measured the growth rate at about a meter of increased radius per year. Within this area, the planet is cold and lifeless. The atmosphere is barely breathable, even with breath masks. Scholars among the Jedi study the area and speculate on what is killing the planet.

Civilization

After the Dark Jedi Conflict, the Jedi Council on Coruscant established a small school on Almas. The institution was

established on the opposide side of the planet from the Sith fortress so that Jedi could monitor it from a distance. Soon new Jedi came to be trained, and a Jedi academy was established. Nerra Ziveri, a Twi'lek Jedi Master, believed that the fortress would be important to the future of the galaxy in some way and devoted his energies to probing it. Around his school, a town grew.

Forard, as the town was named, was built right on top of a massive patch of kaluthin grass. The presence of buildings does not seem to have adversely affected the plants' growth. The town primarily serves the academy. As such, it provides some entertainment facilities and basic services, but very little else. Those who are not training in the Jedi arts are not permitted near the academy. This prohibition has affected the town's development. From above, Forard looks like a donut, with the academy at the center.

Forard's governor is a Duros Jedi consular who found teaching far too dull. Klis Joo was trained on Coruscant and came to the academy after Ziveri disappeared. She tried her hand at teaching, but found herself frustrated by her lack of patience with the students. When the former governor of Forard died, she stepped in and assumed control. She has proven an able administrator and has made significant improvements in the town.

Forard boasts a small spaceship landing field and minimal starship services. Klis Joo brought an experienced starship mechanic in and upgraded the landing facilities. Now the field can manage twenty ships at a time, an improvement over the four it could handle when Joo became governor.

Buildings in the town are sealed from the planet's atmosphere. Residents do not need breath masks in their homes; instead, they can adjust the richness of the air using atmospheric regulators. Each building is separately adjustable.

Although Forard exists primarily because of the academy, it still boasts a population of nearly twenty-four thousand. The planet's strange lighting and peaceful isolation draw a number of beings who have nothing at all to do with the Jedi. Among the population one can find a few thousand droids, but the kaluthin-covered ground hampers their movement. Most droids are tracked; they're used for agricultural labor or loading and unloading. The limited police force uses droids for enforcement and investigation. Droids are not affected by the mind tricks of Jedi, or potential Dark Jedi. Each one has been equipped with a device that broadcasts a signal when the droid is rendered inoperative for any reason, alerting the police to its location. Police respond to a downed security droid very quickly. A squad of officers can reach anywhere in the town within two minutes. Because of the Jedi, there is little crime here, but for the same reason, certain types of crimes that do not draw attention are easy to perpetrate in Forard.

A research station stands on the outskirts of the city. This station's sole purpose is to study the kaluthin and determine whether they can be transplanted to other planets. Three years of study, however, have failed to bring the science team

any answers. The sponsors, a consortium of universities in the Core Worlds, continue to send graduate students and experts, despite the lack of results. In some ways, this isolated research location is a kind of punishment for the senior scientists assigned there. In another way, it is a desirable posting. It all depends on what one wants in one's career.

The station has three levels below the surface of Almas and four above. It is built so that kaluthin actually grow into the floor of the facility, providing natural lighting. In the lower levels, the kaluthin roots are studied, alien plants are cross-pollinated with the kaluthin, and some darker experiments are conducted without the knowledge of the senior scientists.

Klis Joo

Born in the orbiting cities of Duros, Klis proved as adept with technology as any of her race. However, a visiting Jedi sensed that the Force was strong with her. He brought her to Coruscant to train as a Jedi. The famed Duros calm was not always her ally, but she displayed enough persistence for three Duroses. She finally became a Jedi Knight and returned to her homeworld to serve her people. She found, after a short time, that she no longer belonged there. She was different, and her people treated her as if she were royalty rather than one of them. When she could not stand this treatment any longer, she left.

Nerra Ziveri, who had known her when she was in training, invited her to come to his academy and pass on what she had learned. Having no other options, she agreed. She found her true place not among the students, but in the town.

Short for a Duros, Klis nonetheless looks very typical of her species. Her blue skin stands out among the Humans of the town, and even among the Tarasin. She is not particularly attractive, especially to Humans. She hotly defies anyone who calls her a Neimoidian. Klis proudly points out that her species, instead of cheating everyone it comes into contact with, serves the galaxy by piloting and building starships.

Klis herself is short-tempered for a Duros, which is to say that she has the temper of a normal Human. She thrives at improving things and wants to build the town into something special. What that is, she does not know. She continues to use her Jedi powers, but has fallen out of the habit of listening for the will of the Force. She loves to tinker with starships. Her current hobby involves building a racer for the Eskaron Games.

Klis Joo: Female Duros Jedi Consular 10: Init +2; Defense 19 (+7 class, +2 Dex); Spd 10 m; VP/WP 51/12; Atk +9/+4 melee (3d8, lightsaber), +9/+4 ranged (3d6, blaster pistol); SV Fort +8, Ref +7, Will +9; SZ M; FP 9; Rep 6; Str 10, Dex 14, Con 12, Int 16, Wis 15, Cha 9.

Skills: Computer Use +14, Craft (starship) +12, Knowledge (bureaucracy) +11, Knowledge (Cularin system) +7, Knowledge (Jedi lore) +9, Pilot +7, Repair +9, Sense Motive +6, Treat Injury +4; Read/Write Basic, Speak Basic, Speak Tarasinese.

Force Skills: Empathy +7, Enhance Ability +9, Enhance Senses +9, Friendship +5, Move Object +9, See Force +10, Telepathy +6.

Feats: Exotic Weapon Proficiency (lightsaber), Skill Emphasis (Craft [starship]), Starship Operation (space transports), Weapon Finesse (lightsaber), Weapon Group Proficiencies (blaster pistols, simple weapons).

Force Feats: Alter, Burst of Speed, Control, Force Mastery, Force-Sensitive, Sense.

Bran Isken

Bran Isken, a native of Corellia, was born on a starship and learned to repair it as a child. The son of a smuggler, he found a high demand for his rapidly growing skill as an expert technician. Instead of taking to legitimate business, he became a contact smugglers and pirates could go to for repairs on the sly, and for modifications that were not strictly legal. He could also forge new ship identifications and configure ships to hide illegal components. During his later years, while repairing a ship for some Duros, he met Klis. When she needed a mechanic and invited him to Almas, he came willingly.

Thin and dark-haired, he still manages to look rakish. Most of the time, he wears overalls. He prefers a combat flightsuit when he's wary of legal entanglements. His beard is thin and patchy, but people tend to focus on his cybernetic eye instead of the flaws in his beard. Nearing 60 years old, he has taken to dyeing his hair to retain his youthful appearance.

Bran is friendly but suspicious, always willing to "do a favor." He stores up favors in return and has surprised clients on occasion by asking for something unexpected. Because of his extensive contacts with smugglers and pirates, he can be counted on to acquire whatever piece of technology he cannot build, usually within a few standard weeks. He enjoys his life and enjoys his position on Almas. He still works on smuggler vessels on the side, but the Jedi do not seem to mind. Nirama has tried to lure him away twice, but the situation on Almas is much safer.

Bran Isken: Male Human Expert 15; Init +3; Defense 18 (+5 class, +3 Dex); Spd 10 m; WP 10; Atk +12/+7/+2 melee (2d4, vibrodagger), +14/+9/+4 ranged (3d8, heavy blaster pistol); SV Fort +5, Ref +8, Will +10; SZ M; FP 3; Rep 6; Str 12, Dex 17, Con 10, Int 14, Wis 12, Cha 13.

Equipment: Very extensive starship tool kit, starship construction tools, eight astromech droids.

Skills: Astrogate +11, Computer Use +20, Craft (engineering—droids) +14, Craft (electronics—security systems) +19, Craft (starship) +20, Disable Device +15, Forgery +20, Gather Information +11, Hide +10, Knowledge (engineering—security systems) +19, Listen +3, Pilot +10, Repair +25, Sense Motive +9, Spot +2; Read/Write Basic, Speak Basic.

Feats: Force-Sensitive, Gearhead, Sharp-Eyed, Skill Emphasis (Forgery), Skill Emphasis (Repair), Weapon Group Proficiencies (blaster pistols, simple weapons, vibro weapons).

Gilloma

An Ithorian, Gilloma was attracted strongly to kaluthin research. He is only a junior scientist at the research facility, but he does not mind. He has never put himself forward, and positions of prominence have always seemed to pass him by. At first he wished for fame, but he then came to realize that grants and policies did not distract him from his work. He attended the University of Alderaan, taught there for more than twelve years, and then transferred to Almas when he became tired of students who were slow to understand his teaching. Now he heads the project to crossbreed kaluthin with plants native to other worlds, finding this work satisfying, yet frustrating.

He stands nearly two meters tall. His hammerhead snout makes him appear even taller. Despite his imposing height, his appearance is not noteworthy. He looks plain, dresses plainer, and remains quiet most of the time. His real zeal is reserved for his plant research. He hopes to revolutionize the use of plants throughout the galaxy.

Gilloma: Male Ithorian Expert 10; Init +0; Defense 13 (+3 class); Spd 10 m; WP 9; Atk +7/+2 ranged (3d6, blaster pistol); SV Fort +2, Ref +3, Will +7; SZ M; Rep 2; Str 10, Dex 11, Con 9, Int 17, Wis 10, Cha 11.

Skills: Computer Use +15, Diplomacy +3, Gather Information +12, Knowledge (alien species—Tarasin) +11, Knowledge (life sciences) +18, Knowledge (physical sciences—chemistry) +13, Knowledge (Cularin system—flora) +13, Listen +5, Profession (educator) +9, Search +10, Spot +5; Read/Write Ithorese, R/W Basic, Speak Ithorese, Speak Basic.

Feats: Low Profile, Sharp-Eyed, Skill Emphasis (Knowledge [life sciences]), Weapon Group Proficiencies (blaster pistols, simple weapons).

S2P-030

OhThreeOh is basically a rolling computer with arms. His arms extend from the front of his massive box of a body. Both are equipped with tool mounts for various tasks. OhThreeOh is ostensibly programmed for botanical research. He collects samples and makes tests in conditions that are dangerous for living beings. His voice comes from somewhere inside his frame; he does not have a face or mouth. His visual sensors are mounted front and back, giving him 360-degree vision.

A little stiff, OhThreeOh mingles with the researchers as much as possible, but does not interact with them unless required to do so. His completely Non-Human appearance makes it easier for the researchers to see him as a machine. In truth, his relative invisibility makes him perfect for his secondary function. OhThreeOh is an espionage droid. He records whatever he sees and periodically broadcasts reports on the progress of research into space, usually toward Genarius. He does not know who programmed him to do this, or even that he does it, but he is programmed to avoid detection.

S2P-030: Wheeled Research Droid Expert 9; Init +0; Defense 13 (+3 class); Spd 8 m; WP 11; Atk +6/+1 melee

and ranged (no weapons); SV Fort +3, Ref +3, Will +6; SZ M; Rep 1; Str 10, Dex 10, Con 11, Int 17, Wis 10, Cha 11.

Equipment: Vocabulator, two extendable arms, telescopic vision, tool mounts on arms, internal storage (2 kg), environmental compensator, recording unit (audio and video), internal hidden comlink.

Skills: Computer Use +18, Gather Information +10, Knowledge (Cularin system–flora) +15, Knowledge (life sciences) +15, Listen +15, Repair +7, Search +13, Spot +9; Speak Basic.

Feats: Low Profile, Skill Emphasis (Computer Use), Skill Emphasis (Listen), Skill Emphasis (Search).

Dorumaa

> ### Dorumaa at a Glance
> **Type:** Terraformed terrestrial
> **Climate:** Oceans, small continents
> **Length of Day:** 28 standard hours
> **Length of Year:** 8,784 standard days

The resort moon of Dorumaa, like so many other planets and moons throughout the galaxy, would be utterly uninhabitable were it not for terraforming technology. Until fifteen years ago, Dorumaa was little more than a huge chunk of ice orbiting Almas. Now it has become one of the more popular tourist attractions in the Mid Rim, and it's certainly the most popular one in all of the Cularin system.

The origins of Dorumaa are unclear. The atmosphere of the planet is thick enough with critical elements that it should not have developed this far from the twin suns. Current speculation is that Dorumaa was once an inner planet in the system. When a massive impact knocked it out of its orbit, it settled into an orbit over Almas. This theory is correct. A planet once traveled through an orbit where the asteroid field is now; occasionally, it crossed orbits with Dorumaa. They were at their closest point ever when the explosion occurred, sending Dorumaa out away from the suns. The rain of debris slowed down the planet's progress and allowed it to settle into orbit above Almas, rather than smashing into it. After its traumatic exit from its orbit, Dorumaa's distance from the suns flash-froze the fresh water seas on the surface of the planet, along with everything that lived below.

To make Dorumaa habitable, large holes were drilled through the thick layer of ice. Near the core of the moon, power generators were constructed to warm the planet and recycle the atmosphere. Gravity generators were built to bring the gravity closer to galactic standard. When the generators were turned on, the atmosphere warmed, and the ice melted into expansive crystal-blue oceans stretching over eighty-five percent of the moon's surface. Scientists quickly terraformed the other fifteen percent of the surface into tropical islands, and construction began on the resorts.

Unbeknownst to the Dorumaa Investment Group, trouble was brewing beneath the oceans. Because of the volume of dead creatures that floated to the surface—some of them fish the size of sail barges—the company's officers assumed anything that might have lived there was long since dead. Unfortunately, they were wrong. Any creature that had been living at the moment of the explosion died when the seas flash-froze. However, many of the life forms had laid eggs in the sea floor during the cold portion of the year before the explosion. As the seas thawed and grew warmer, nutrients began feeding those frozen eggs, and the slow thaw brought them back to life. The indigenous creatures of Dorumaa were reborn. While the investors have turned this into a marketing tool, even the senior investors sometimes worry about what may lie beneath the waves.

On occasion, vacationers rent boats in the morning, and never return in the evening. When this happens, their families receive a massive financial settlement, and no one ever hears a word from them again.

El'Tar Miskin

El'Tar Miskin is the Human concierge at Greentree Pointe, a family-oriented resort island located thirty degrees north of Dorumaa's equator. El'Tar is a young man (as are most of the staff on Dorumaa) with a ready smile and a penchant for rubbing his hands together anxiously while he talks. Before coming to Dorumaa, he worked as a shipping clerk for Naescorcom and was fired for negligence. While stories about his removal vary considerably, it appears that he mixed up a pair of shipments going to very different customers. The pirates from the Outer Rim were somewhat surprised to open their crates and find a shipment of high-quality textiles, but not nearly as surprised as the orphanage on Coruscant that received five cases of thermal detonators!

His affable nature kept him from being killed for the blunder. El'Tar quickly moved on to other venues. He is happy on Dorumaa, since the work gives him opportunities to interact with people, including extremely rich and influential people. He has designs on starting his own business, hoping that if he can impress enough of the wealthy members of galactic society with his skill, charm, and knowledge of Dorumaa, he can secure funding. Exactly what kind of business he wants to start remains unclear—even to El'Tar—but he is quite confident it will be a success.

El'Tar Miskin: Male Human Expert 5; Init +1; Defense 12 (+1 class, +1 Dex); Spd 10 m; WP 12; Atk +4 ranged (3d6, blaster pistol); SV Fort +4, Ref +2, Will +5; SZ M; Rep 1; Str 11, Dex 13, Con 12, Int 14, Wis 13, Cha 16.

Skills: Bluff +6, Computer Use +6, Diplomacy +9, Knowledge (business) +7, Knowledge (Cularin system) +5, Knowledge (spacer lore) +6, Profession (hotel staff) +4, Profession (clerk) +7, Sense Motive +3, Treat Injury +3; Read/Write Basic, R/W Sullustese, Speak Basic, Speak Sullustese, Speak Tarasinese.

Feats: Alertness, Great Fortitude, Trustworthy, Weapon Group Proficiency (simple weapons).

Rena Laut

Rena is a middle-aged Human woman who rents boats (technically, low-riding skiffs designed to travel over water) to Dorumaa's visitors. Her hair has been sun-bleached blonde from years spent on the surface of Cularin doing missionary work among the Tarasin. (Outdoor tanning is impossible on Dorumaa, given its distance from the suns.) Her skin is coarse and leathery. She hardly ever smiles, but laughs frequently, sometimes at strange or inappropriate moments.

Given the amount of time she's put into learning the seas of Dorumaa, Rena has some very definite opinions about what lives down there. "See, here's the thing. What you got is a lot of water. Lots of things live out there. Some of them aren't too nice. So, what you got to do is just expect that when you go out, you may not be coming back. Not that I expect anything bad to happen to you, since if I did, you wouldn't be taking my boat with you. But if something were to happen, I've gotta tell you, it wouldn't be the first time. Especially since you may not know everything there is to know about how to pilot one of my boats. Now, did you say you wanted a guide for this little trip, or no?"

Rena's rates are reasonable, even if her sales pitch isn't,

and she does worry about her customers—almost as much as she worries about her boats.

Rena Laut: Female Human Expert 3; Init +0; Defense 11 (+1 class); Spd 10 m; WP 9; Atk +2 ranged (3d6, blaster pistol); SV Fort +0, Ref +1, Will +5; SZ M; Rep 0; Str 11, Dex 10, Con 9, Int 13, Wis 14, Cha 12.

Skills: Knowledge (Dorumaa system—seas) +7, Knowledge (Cularin system) +5, Pilot +9, Survival +5, Spot +3, Treat Injury +5; Read/Write Basic, Speak Basic.

Feats: Alertness, Dodge, Skill Emphasis (Pilot), Weapon Group Proficiency (simple weapons).

Sarken Rimk

Rimk is a Gungan diving instructor who operates a small business out of his home on the coast of Whitesand Island. He is not terribly patient and tends to forget that not every species is built for aquatic life. He flips his ears irritably whenever someone really begins to grate on his nerves. He often mutters insults under his breath when he thinks no one is listening.

He is Force-Sensitive, although this is a fact he hesitates to share with anyone else, since it provides him an advantage in dealing with customers. Regardless whether they've learned anything important about diving, every customer leaves with the belief that they've learned a great deal, and they tip appropriately.

Sarken Rimk: Male Gungan Expert 4; Init +0; Defense 11 (+1 class); Spd 10 m; WP 9; Atk +3 ranged (3d6, blaster pistol); SV Fort +2, Ref +1, Will +3; SZ M; Rep 0; Str 15, Dex 10, Con 12, Int 13, Wis 9, Cha 10.

Skills: Jump +1, Knowledge (Dorumaa) +4, Knowledge (Cularin system) +1, Profession (teacher) +3, Repair +2, Spot +3, Survival +4, Swim +12; Read/Write Basic, Speak Basic.

Feats: Athletic, Skill Emphasis (Swim), Weapon Group Proficiency (simple weapons).

Drac Gerrat

Drac Gerrat operates a fishing boat in which he roams the seas. He can be found in almost any bar on Dorumaa at one time or another, sharing stories from his travels. His ultimate goal is to kill a Nus Whale and sell polished fragments of its bones, marketing them as good luck charms. For the time being, he avoids the whales altogether, since the bulls could swallow his ship, the *Icon*, in a single gulp.

Drac Gerrat: Male Human Soldier 7; Init +3; Defense 17 (+4 class, +3 Dex); Spd 10 m; VP/WP 67/17; Atk +10/+5 ranged (3d6, blaster pistol); SV Fort +8, Ref +7, Will +4; SZ M; Rep 0; FP 3; Str 17, Dex 16, Con 17, Int 15, Wis 14, Cha 11.

Skills: Astrogate +9, Demolitions +10, Hide +6, Intimidate +5, Knowledge (culture—military) +10, Knowledge (galactic politics) +9, Knowledge (streetwise—Coruscant) +7, Listen +6, Pilot +9, Repair +7, Spot +7, Treat Injury +5; Read/Write Basic, Speak Basic.

Feats: Alertness, Armor Proficiencies (light, medium, heavy), Far Shot, Lightning Reflexes, Point Blank Shot, Quickness, Weapon Focus (blaster pistol), Weapon Focus (blaster rifle), Weapon Group Proficiencies (blaster pistols, blaster rifles, heavy weapons, simple weapons, vibro weapons).

Management

Dorumaa Resort is operated by a group of Humans, Gungans, and Twi'leks so cheerful they are jokingly referred to as "Neo-Caarites." Service with a smile is a way of life on Dorumaa. If the customer is ever wrong, management makes changes to ensure that the customer is right.

The Head Manager for Dorumaa is Mar Daghreb. A set of five property managers report to Mar, each of whom has five individuals reporting to him as well. Dorumaa Investment Group research indicated that the optimal span of control within resort communities was five individuals, since having more than that reporting to a single person results in too little time for, and attention to, the guests. All of the managers possess the same "public face" as Mar, but none of them have a private temper to match hers.

Mar Daghreb

Mar, a Human woman in her late twenties, has a dark complexion and wears her long black hair pulled back in a loose ponytail. She is able to make every person who meets

her feel important, and she is personally responsible for much of Dorumaa's return business. She goes out of her way to "sell" the resort to its visitors. The beautiful scenery, combined with her charm and wit, keep them coming back.

Her relations with the staff are somewhat more strained. With the guests, she is all smiles and handshakes, vivaciously tossing her ponytail. Away from the guests, she turns into a harsh, unyielding, brutally honest woman with fire in her eyes. She does not tolerate incompetence, and she will release an employee at the first sign of malfeasance rather than risk sullying the reputation of her resort. She can then turn around and be as sweet as Cularin sugarcane to the next employee in line. Her ability to switch between a rational, reasonable boss and a "screaming beast-woman," as the employees call her behind her back, keeps the staff on their toes.

Mar Daghreb: Female Human Expert 8; Init +2; Defense 14 (+2 class, +2 Dex); Spd 10 m; WP 11; Atk +8/+3 ranged (3d6, blaster pistol); SV Fort +2, Ref +4, Will +6; SZ M; Rep 4; Str 12, Dex 15, Con 11, Int 15, Wis 11, Cha 15.

Skills: Appraise +8, Bluff +8, Computer Use +5, Diplomacy +10, Gather Information +9, Knowledge (business) +14, Knowledge (Cularin system) +11, Knowledge (galactic society) +8, Profession (resort manager) +10, Sense Motive +6; Read/Write Basic, Speak Basic.

Feats: Persuasive, Sharp-Eyed, Skill Emphasis (Diplomacy), Skill Emphasis (Knowledge [business]), Weapon Group Proficiency (simple weapons).

Investors

The Dorumaa Investment Group is a local consortium that includes SoroSuub and the other major powers of Genarius, as well as investors from trading houses on Cularin and other planets throughout the system. Most of the voting on issues is done via proxies, who are in constant contact with their employers during critical meetings. Because operations on Dorumaa have never been guaranteed to be either profitable or safe, many of the investors choose to remain anonymous, making numbered contributions to the DIG accounts to indicate their support for Dorumaa's progress. Withdrawals from those accounts are carefully monitored using the same numbers to represent investors. Names are never used.

Recently, the investments from Identification #43641, a newer consortium member, have increased dramatically. This has allowed a floating landing pad to be established in the center of the sea, as far from the islands as possible, per #43641's instructions. Ostensibly, the pad is designed as an easy dropoff point for deep-sea fishing, but no boats have ever been seen in the area. The only ships that use the pad do so at night. Individuals of the paranoid, speculative type tend to wonder aloud whether #43641's entry to the consortium may have coincided a bit too closely with the Republic military establishing a presence in the system.

Lifeforms

The creatures that hatched far beneath the fresh water seas struggled at first. More than half died. The rest fought, struggled, and survived.

The indigenous life forms evolved with shorter life spans because of the traumatic changes in seasons in Dorumaa's former orbit. The hardiest creatures lived more than three or four years. A few whalelike creatures the size of sail barges floated to the surface when the seas thawed, and all were about that age. Now, after five years of stable climate, the seas are teeming with life, in sizes and quantities never before seen in the species.

A year's growth for the great Nus Whale can be in the neighborhood of twenty meters when food is plentiful. Currently, a herd of Nus Whales are crisscrossing the sea floor, scavenging food and growing absolutely enormous. There are at least ten bulls of at least 100 meters in length, and twelve cows of 80 to 90 meters. The fertilized eggs were buried somewhere in the deep ocean two springs ago. The Nus herd will return to that spot next spring to retrieve the newborn calves.

Other fish, some perfect for sport fishing, have revived in the waters of Dorumaa as well. Giant sea turtles hatched in the shallows off Greentree Pointe early this summer, much to the surprise of children who believed they were playing on large rocks. The turtles are friendly creatures who enjoy playing with the small Humans, often giving them rides out into the ocean. While no harnesses fit the creatures, none have ever been necessary. Children and adults alike are taken for rides by the turtles and brought back unharmed.

Morjakar

> ### Morjakar at a Glance
> Type: Craggy barren rock
> Climate: None
> Length of Day: 18 standard hours
> Length of Year: 1,140 standard days

The planetoid of Morjakar does not really belong to the Cularin system. Morjakar's origins can be traced (if possible) to a very old system half a galaxy away. The sun of that system turned into a red giant and destroyed the planets. Morjakar was the farthest terrestrial planet from the sun. Instead of being consumed, it was somehow thrown from the system. Cast adrift, it wandered for thousands of years, eventually passing the fledgling Cularin system. The heavy gravity of the planets and the two suns attracted it into an eccentric orbit, and there it has remained. While the rest of the planets have orbits that all lie in a plane (more or less), Morjakar's orbit lies at an angle of about 50 degrees relative to that plane. It travels far from the suns, then comes back and passes through the system's plane somewhere between the orbits of Acilaris and Cularin. So far, the passing of Morjakar has never caused major seismic disruption to

Cularin, but eventually it must do so.

The planetoid does not support an atmosphere of any kind. The minerals that make up the rocky crust are common, but no one has bothered to make a proper survey. When Reidi Artom discovered the system, Morjakar was drifting away from the suns. She did not realize that the planet even existed. When it returned, people were more interested in its orbit than its composition. Two brief surveys were made in later years, but the results were inconclusive. The brief surveys did not discover any traces of civilization on the planetoid, but a more proper survey might reveal some of Morjakar's unknown past.

Power Groups in Cularin

Interest in Cularin runs high, and several powerful groups operate within the system. These groups influence the lives of almost everyone to some degree. They can manipulate the fate of the whole system. The most powerful groups operating in Cularin are presented here.

Metatheran Cartel

The Metatheran Cartel is composed of two main species, the Caarites and the Filordi. Meeting in secret on Filordis, the Caarites persuaded the Filordi to withdraw from the Trade Federation and join them in a new venture. With broad, ingratiating smiles, the Caarites claimed the Trade Federation was doomed. To some extent, they were right. With the departure of the Neimoidians, the Metatheran Cartel became the dominant trade group in the Cularin system.

Like the Trade Federation before them, the Cartel operates with ruthlessly expedient policies. The leaders of the Cartel believe that low costs and high profits make for the best businesses. To reach that goal, they will manipulate, control, and monopolize any field of trade or manufacture that can turn a profit. The best way to do business in a system is by dominating it and forcing it into submission.

The Cartel is cautious not to exercise too much control too quickly. Alienating the inhabitants of a system before businesses are fully entrenched there sets a bad business relationship. Unfortunately, their corporations are firmly established on Cularin. They forced out the Trade Federation by using the Neimoidians' own methods against them, and they will not hesistate to use those same tactics again. As former members of the Trade Federation, they developed many of its shadier business practices, making a healthy profit by doing so.

The Metatheran Cartel maintains close ties with several other corporations, including the SoroSuub Corporation and Sienar Fleet Systems. These partners are not full Cartel members, but enjoy preferential trade status. The Cartel's main operations are centered in the Cularin system. It also

Caarites

Caarites are sly, ingratiating beings whose penchant for crooked dealings is cloaked by their friendly demeanors. While they suffer from a rather poor reputation, it is difficult for anyone around a Caarite for an extended period of time to believe it is capable of anything truly malicious. They wear broad grins, bearing a double row of wide, flat, perfectly white teeth. Taking advantage of their frail, friendly appearance, they seize the upper hand in negotiations, exuding an almost childlike charm when dealing directly with large groups of individuals.

Personality: Friendly, entertaining, humorous, but filled with a desire to get the better of their rivals by any means necessary.

Physical Description: Caarites are about a meter tall, with features that are vaguely porcine. While basically humanoid, they have slightly elongated snouts turned delicately upward at their tips. Their broad, open faces make their open smiles look even friendlier. Their flesh is pale pink, and they are completely hairless.

Caarite Homeworld: The Outer Rim planet of Caarimon is a warm, saunalike planet with great humidity.

Language: Caarites speak Caarimala and Basic. Each knows at least one additional language.

Example Names: Velin Wir, Thurm Loogg.

Adventurers: Caarites who become adventurers do so for personal gain. They favor nonviolent means when face-to-face with an adversary, but they nonetheless carry a number of tools and ranged weapons. Caarites favor the scoundrel and fringer classes. Because they are averse to physical combat, they do not take up the

continued on page 45

maintains facilities on the homeworlds of its member species. Activity in Cularin has been light in the past year, but the Cartel is now ready to exert its full influence.

The Cartel's best-known spokesman, Thurm Loogg, heads the offices on Cularin and oversees mining operations on Tilnes. Loogg acts as a diplomat and facilitator. Despite his position, the Cartel leaders do not expect him to conduct any real business. Instead, the Cartel leaders pursue individual agendas. They don't purposefully act against each other, but they have little regard for the group's long-term success. It wouldn't be surprising to find several Filordi engaged in some business enterprise to further their terraforming plans, unaware that a Caarite group is conducting business at cross-purposes. When these oversights become public knowledge, Loogg has to step in and preserve the Cartel's public image.

The Metatheran Cartel conducts legitimate business, but occasionally it bypasses its own trade regulations by hiring smugglers to bring in illicit goods. In addition to making extra money, the Cartel keeps tabs on its main competition by sponsoring smugglers. Some of the leaders also make occasional deals with pirates. These either involve harassment of legitimate shipping or strikes against smugglers to keep them weak. Some people on Cularin think that the Cartel is

behind every nefarious activity that takes place. Due to the diverse activities of the various Cartel members, these ideas are more correct than most citizens realize.

Thurm Loogg

As the Metatheran Cartel envoy to Cularin, Thurm is unclear about what he's supposed to be doing there. The Cartel recently began to increase its presence on Cularin because of plentiful minerals and rare woods, but it has failed to keep Loogg informed of all their plans. Thus, he tries to represent the Cartel in talks without really knowing what his superiors expect of him. He continues this façade because he only wants one thing—credits—and he's willing to do whatever it takes to get them. He'll beg, borrow, steal, or kill (or have others do the killing) it he can score a bit of profit. His policies tend to favor his own interests. Satisfying the unspoken desires of the Cartel leaders usually furthers his own greed.

Thurm has an ingratiating whine common to most Caarites, along with the species' broad, toothy smile. He always dresses in dark blue robes trimmed in red. He talks with his hands a great deal and ignores anything he doesn't want to hear, often waving people off in mid-sentence. He is frustrating to deal with because he's the embodiment of

44

everything that's wrong with the Cartel's policies. Things will be done his way, at his price, on his schedule, or they won't be done at all.

Thurm Loogg: Male Caarite Diplomat 7; Init +1; Defense 14 (+2 class, +1 Dex, +1 size); Spd 6m; WP 8; Atk +4 ranged (3d6, blaster pistol); SV Fort +1, Ref +2, Will +6; SZ S; FP 1; Rep 2; Str 11, Dex 12, Con 8, Int 15, Wis 13, Cha 16.

  Equipment: Protocol droid (BR-3PO).

  Skills: Bluff +16, Diplomacy +14, Gather Information +11, Knowledge (Cularin system) +10, Knowledge (business) +11, Sense Motive +11; Read/Write Caarimala, Read/Write Basic, Read/Write Huttese, Read/Write Rodian, Speak Basic, Speak Caarimala, Speak Tarasinese, Speak Rodian, Speak Twi'lek, Speak Huttese.

Feats: Persuasive, Skill Emphasis (Bluff), Trustworthy, Weapon Group Proficiency (simple weapons).

Organized Crime

Smuggling, piracy, loansharking, blackmail—the organized criminals of the Cularin system engage in just about anything likely to turn a profit. They take advantage of the relative isolation of their system, acting with a boldness not seen anywhere else outside the Outer Rim territories.

When Riboga the Hutt came to the Cularin system more than eighty standard years ago, he settled on Cularin itself and began building his organization. Importing outsiders as enforcers and key administrative personnel, he soon had his grubby digits in every type of crime that could be imagined, including slavery.

CAARITES AND FILORDI

continued from page 44

soldier class. Some Caarites are Force-Sensitive, but their inherent greed prevents them from truly embracing the way of the Jedi.

Caarite Species Traits

- ↻ +2 Charisma, -2 Constitution. Caarites are very friendly and persuasive, but not very sturdy.
- ↻ Small. As Small creatures, Caarites gain a +1 size bonus to their Defense, a +1 size bonus on attack rolls, and a +4 size bonus on Hide checks. They must use smaller weapons than Humans use, and their lifting and carrying limits are three-quarters those of Medium-size characters.
- ↻ Caarite base speed is 6 meters.
- ↻ +2 species bonus to Survival checks in hot climates; −2 species penalty to Survival checks in cold climates.
- ↻ Automatic Languages: Caarimala and Basic.

Filordi

Filordi care about two things: making their homeworld less hostile, and getting away from it. Some Filordi prefer to make what they can of their homeworld; thus, they have begun terraforming in earnest. Hardy and intelligent, a Filordus adapts to whatever circumstances it finds itself in, at least for the moment. Filordi are driven to succeed, but seem incapable of planning for long-term success. In this way, they are a short-sighted species. To survive, they consume every bit of any resource that comes their way. Frequently the best way to defeat a Filordi is to give it what it wants, then leave before it changes its mind. Filordi are asexual; they reproduce while dying. A week after its host has died, an infant Filordi crawls from the corpse of its predecessor.

  Personality: Persistent, resourceful, creative, and ruthlessly opportunistic.

  Physical Description: About 1.4 meters tall, Filordi have six limbs: they're two-armed quadrupeds. Two arms hang from a Filordus's shoulders. Long, spindly front legs grow from its abominal area. Shorter stubby back legs extend from its hindquarters. Both legs have pincer toes and flat feet—the pincers face rearward on the front legs and forward on the back legs. In a brawl, a Filordus usually crouches on its hind legs, fighting with its arms and pincers.

Filordi can rise up and walk in bipedal fashion, but this is very tiring. Their faces are humanoid. Their large ears can fold down over their eyes to protect them from wind and rain. Their bodies are covered in light-colored short hair, sometimes marked with stripes of blue.

  Filordi Homeworld: Filordis, a world circling a red star, is a rocky wasteland with fierce winds and frequent thunderstorms.

  Language: Filordi speak Filordian. They can speak Basic with gravely voices that miss some of the consonant sounds.

  Example Names: Grizztil, Furran, Hizkal.

  Adventurers: Filordi leave their homeworld to find better places to live. Most places are better than their homeworld, so they can be found almost anywhere. Once out in the galaxy, they dabble in many different pursuits, largely because they cannot focus on any one pursuit at great length. There are very few Filordi nobles, and no Force adepts among them. They take up all other classes. A few have even been trained as Jedi.

Filordi Species Traits

- ↻ +2 Constitution, -2 Dexterity. Filordi are hardy, but not graceful. Coordinating their six limbs takes considerable effort.
- ↻ Medium-size. As Medium-size creatures, Filordi have no species bonuses or penalties due to their size.
- ↻ Filordi base speed is 14 meters. With their four legs, they can move very quickly. When bipedal, their base speed drops to 6 meters.
- ↻ Natural pincer attack with two back leg pincers: 1d6 points of damage per pincer.
- ↻ +4 species bonus to Listen checks. With their huge ears, Filordi are used to picking out sounds from the howling winds of their homeworld.
- ↻ −2 species penalty to Fortitude saves against sonic attacks. Big ears have drawbacks.
- ↻ Automatic Language: Filordian.

45

For some years, he fought with the so-called Smuggler's Confederation. The smugglers originally organized their "guild" to gain better access to jobs. When the Smuggler's Confederation elected a new leader seventy-nine standard years ago, Riboga entered into a deal to absorb the network into his own organization, rather like a corporate acquisition. To most smugglers, this change in leadership meant nothing to their day-to-day activities. The smugglers themselves still retain the old name when referring to themselves as a group. In reality, the smugglers are all bound to Riboga's organization in one way or another.

To further cement these bonds, Riboga loaned the more recalcitrant smugglers money to upgrade their ships. The interest rates were exorbitant, but the Hutt did offer an alternative. In return for lowering the interest rates to levels the smugglers could afford, he accepted contracts for their services for set periods of time. Throughout the years, Riboga continued to offer these contracts and loans to bind successful criminals to his organization.

Struggles with the asteroid-based pirates plagued Riboga for many years, but Riboga learned from their methods. After about fifteen standard years of operation on Cularin, he created a secret asteroid base for his systemwide criminal operations. The base, which took two years to complete, is a shrine to efficiency and Hutt extravagance. It even contains a bathing pool for Hutts and a breeding chamber.

Because of his notoriety, Riboga knew that he could not operate from a secret base all the time and have it remain secret. After the secret base was completed, he created a more public base of operations in a nearby asteroid. There, he met regularly with smugglers, Trade Federation representatives, and other nefarious guests. The two bases were not always close together, given the properties of asteroid belts, but they usually remained within two planetary diameters of each other.

Liking his comfort, Riboga maintained a residence on Cularin and established an "office" in the floating city of Tolea Biqua, on Genarius. These installations were used more for personal relaxation than business. The Tolea Biqua site was primarily used for spying on potential rivals.

Slavery became one of Riboga's chief businesses forty-six standard years ago, and it remained his most profitable business until his departure. Some Tarasin were abducted, but his main business was the buying, selling, and transport of slaves from outside the system. Slavery was illegal in the Republic, but it was still practiced openly in the Outer Rim, and secretly in the Core Worlds. The semi-isolation of the system created a secure market where slaves could be traded without Republic intervention. Riboga's location allowed him to acquire slaves from the Core Worlds and transport them to the Outer Rim, selling them for a hefty profit in the process. Smugglers would carry the slaves into and out of the Cularin system, but the same smuggler was never used for both trips.

Sometimes slaves were brought insystem on ships with Republic markings.

As the criminal empire grew, an ambitious and capable accountant named Nirama rose to become Riboga's major-domo. He diverted profits from the various enterprises, noting the losses as additional expenses. Report after report that reached Riboga showed that the operations were getting to be much more expensive than he thought. Riboga had several underlings questioned, and even killed, but he could never trace the problem to Nirama. Finally, in one of their regular sabacc games, Riboga mentioned rising prices and the need to curtail some operations. Nirama good-naturedly offered to put up a quarter million credits against the whole operation, and won. Riboga just laughed, took the credits, summoned a few of his most loyal operatives, and returned to Nal Hutta.

Nirama's first act was to end the slave trade Riboga had managed so successfully. Though he engages in a lot of brutal crimes, he does not condone slavery and strikes to eliminate any hint of it within the system. He reorganized the administration, moving less competent and more pliable personnel into positions of power, thus ensuring that no ambitious underling would unseat him. Renewing arrangements with the smugglers and entering into deals with the Trade Federation, he quickly brought the organization back to a very profitable state.

Nirama's current problems revolve around the pirates in the asteroid belt, which neither he nor his predecessor dealt with successfully. He has engaged in some deals with Filordi to acquire technology for them. He has also made a cunning deal with the Republic military to supply parts the pirates continually steal from them. Nirama is beginning to suspect that the parts demanded outweigh the losses from pirates, and he wonders why a colonel of the Republic would go to him for parts that are available legally in most systems.

Most smugglers either act from their ships or from more elaborate asteroid bases. Disliking Nirama as much as Riboga, they very rarely go to the crimelord's base. Instead, they prefer to work through intermediaries or meet Nirama at his residence on Cularin, where they are less likely to have their ships taken from them.

Nirama

The overlord of the smugglers' network in the asteroid belt, Nirama is a vile, disgusting creature. His species comes from the Unknown Regions, and no one has seen another like him. He has a bright pink face with four eyes—two sets, one on top of the other. The top set of eyes are both grayish-blue; the bottom set are as black as night. He has three arms, one at his right shoulder and two at his left. One at his left side points forward while the other points backward—he usually holds a blaster in his rear-facing hand. He has never had to fire it, but its presence discourages sneak attacks.

In spite of his strange appearance and harsh lifestyle, Nirama is not as evil as he may initially appear. He recog-nizes the essential interrelationship of all the beings in the universe, and he doesn't go out of his way to upset that balance. He refuses to allow slavery in the system and is meticulous in the conduct of his business. When people get in his way, he usually makes polite requests that they move aside. When that doesn't work, he kills them.

Nirama: Male Alien Scoundrel 6/Crimelord 9; Init +1; Defense 20 (+9 class, +1 Dex); Spd 10 m; VP/WP 90/15; Atk +8/+3 ranged (3d6, blaster pistol); SA Illicit barter, better lucky than good, sneak attack +2d6, resource access, exceptional minions; SQ Rear hand Dexterity (can use his extra rear-facing arm with a –2 Dex penalty); SV Fort +7, Ref +10, Will +10; SZ M; FP 6; Rep 17; Str 14, Dex 13, Con 15, Int 16, Wis 14, Cha 15.

   Equipment: Blaster pistols, expensive clothing, blast vest hidden near him at all times, personal space yacht *Viper Wing*.

   Skills: Appraise +19, Bluff +20, Computer Use +15, Diplomacy +19, Forgery +18, Gather Information +17, Intimidate +14, Listen +9, Knowledge (alien species—Caarite) +7, Knowledge (Cularin system) +9, Knowledge (streetwise—Cularin system) +12, Pilot +5, Profession (accountant) +10, Search +10, Sense Motive +18, Sleight of Hand +7, Spot +10; Read/Write Basic, Read/Write Caarimala, Read/Write Huttese, Speak Basic, Speak Caarimala, Speak Tarasinese, Speak Huttese, Speak Sullustan.

   Feats: Alertness, Armor Proficiency (light), Infamy, Persuasive, Point Blank Shot, Sharp-Eyed, Skill Emphasis (Forgery), Weapon Group Proficiencies (blaster pistols, simple weapons).

Len Markus

Markus serves as a group representative from the smugglers. Not exactly a second-in-command to Nirama, he nonetheless has a position of power within the criminal's organization. He's a shadowy figure who is more than content to stay in the background and pull strings. While Nirama ostensibly remains in charge, Markus gives most of the orders to the smugglers, placating Nirama with delicacies from faraway galaxies.

Tall and pale, Markus appears more translucent than an average Human. He's not an albino, but he looks very much like one. He generally wears light-colored spacer's clothing when he wants to accentuate his paleness, or darker clothing when he wants to blend in with others. His ready smile is charming and conveys friendship, but does not inspire a great deal of trust or intimacy.

Markus trusts no one, but he is very personable. He instills a belief in those around him that he trusts them implicitly. Although he appears eager to meet associates with backslaps and handshakes, he privately glowers at fools who seem to enjoy such attention. He shifts his position and allegiances, lies through his teeth (with obvious intent), and acts as untrustworthy as a crimelord's aide should be. Nirama finds this behavior amusing. He doesn't care who is giving the

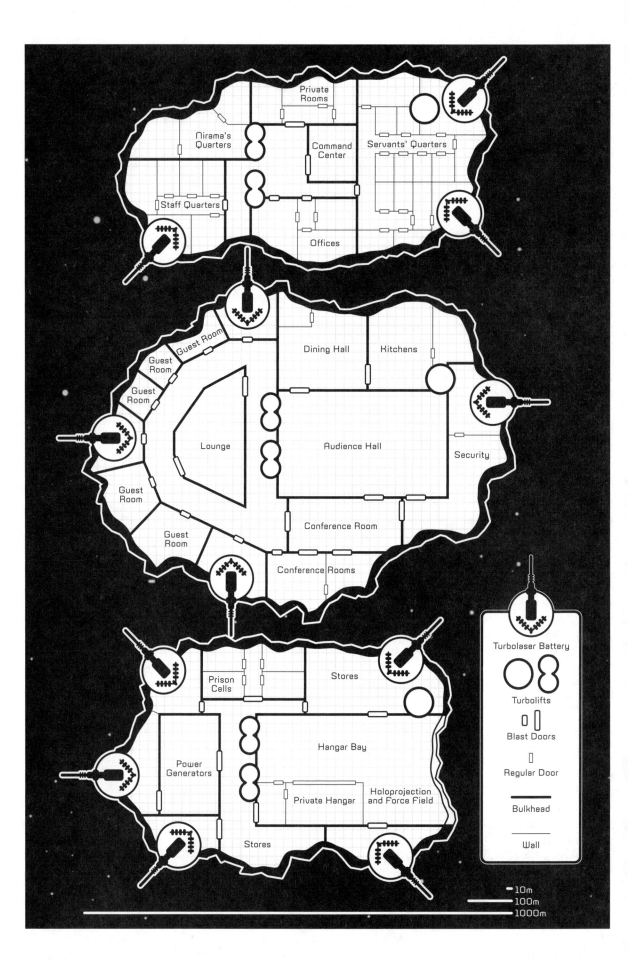

Nirama's Quarters

Private Rooms

Command Center

Servants' Quarters

Staff Quarters

Offices

Guest Room

Guest Room

Guest Room

Dining Hall

Kitchens

Lounge

Audience Hall

Security

Guest Room

Conference Room

Guest Room

Conference Rooms

Prison Cells

Stores

Hangar Bay

Power Generators

Private Hangar

Holoprojection and Force Field

Stores

Turbolaser Battery

Turbolifts

Blast Doors

Regular Door

Bulkhead

Wall

10m
100m
1000m

orders, since he acquired his position in the same way, and he believes he knows exactly how to keep Len Markus in line.

Len Markus: Male Human Fringer 3/Soldier 8; Init +7; Defense 19 (+6 class, +3 Dex); Spd 10 m; VP/WP 79/14; Atk +13/+8 ranged (3d6, blaster pistol); SA Barter, adaptive learning (Tumble); SV Fort +11, Ref +8, Will +5; SZ M; FP 12; Rep 6; Str 13, Dex 17, Con 14, Int 15, Wis 15, Cha 11.

    Equipment: Blaster pistol, lightsaber (carefully concealed).

    Skills: Appraise +4, Computer Use +6, Disguise +3, Hide +5, Intimidate +4, Jump +4, Knowledge (streetwise) +4, Listen +5, Pilot +5, Search +3, Spot +7, Tumble +7; Read/Write Basic, Speak Basic, Speak Sullustan.

    Feats: Alertness, Armor Proficiencies (light, medium, heavy), Blind-Fight, Dodge, Improved Initiative, Low Profile, Quick Draw, Sharp-Eyed, Weapon Group Proficiencies (blaster pistols, blaster rifles, simple weapons, heavy weapons, vibro weapons).

Nadin Paal

Paal serves as the "trade envoy" between Nirama's organization and the planets in the system—he is the spokesman for the organization. A Gran native of Malastare, his three protuberant eyes miss little. He carries a single blaster, always visible at his side, with smaller hold-out blasters hidden in his left sleeve and right boot.

Since the departure of Riboga the Hutt, Nadin has been looking for a way into a more respectable living. He's noticed the increased traffic in the system and knows that trouble is brewing. Unfortunately, Riboga once placed a very large and very conditional bounty on Nadin. As long as Nadin stays in the Cularin system, he is safe, but if he should ever leave, he'll have a death mark on his head. Thus, the Bounty Hunters Guild sends scum to watch Nadin's travels very closely, waiting for the moment when they can finally collect.

Nadin is unsure how to be successful, but he has determined that living in the asteroid belt, smuggling whatever he can get his hands on, is probably not the best way. He's slightly nervous, always looking over his shoulder to make sure no one knows what he's doing. He doesn't want anyone to notice that he's "turning away from" his dark past. When his motives are questioned, he typically gets defensive.

Nadin Paal: Male Gran Scoundrel 8; Init +2; Defense 20 (+8 class, +2 Dex); Spd 10 m; VP/WP 39/13; Atk +8/+3 ranged (3d6, blaster pistol); SA Illicit barter, better lucky than good, sneak attack +2d6; SQ Low-light vision; SV Fort +3, Ref +8, Will +3; SZ M; FP 4; Rep 9; Str 16, Dex 14, Con 13, Int 14, Wis 12, Cha 15.

    Equipment: Blaster pistol, modified YT-1300 space transport *Whirling Stars*.

    Skills: Appraise +7, Astrogate +11, Bluff +12, Computer Use +11, Disable Device +13, Escape Artist +8, Forgery +6, Hide +6, Knowledge (Cularin system) +7, Knowledge (streetwise—Cularin system) +8, Knowledge (spacer lore) +7,

Listen +5, Move Silently +6, Pilot +13, Repair +6, Search +9, Sleight of Hand +7, Spot +6; Read/Write Basic, Speak Basic, Speak Tarasinese, Speak Huttese.

    Feats: Cautious, Skill Emphasis (Disable Device), Skill Emphasis (Computer Use), Starship Dodge (space transports), Starship Operation (space transports), Weapon Group Proficiencies (blaster pistols, simple weapons).

Military Might

When Cularin's first senator was elected, her immediate request was to establish an active military presence in the system. Constant pirate raids on shipping weighed heavily on her mind, but she believed a military base would curb the boldest pirates. The request was approved, but her hope that the pirates would stop died a quick death. The new military presence failed to impress anyone but the senator, the Tarasin, and a few gullible idealists.

Several problems contributed to the ineffectiveness of the intervention. First, the Republic military only authorized a minor presence. With corruption spreading, and skirmishes erupting among member worlds, the Republic couldn't spare major warships and troops for a new base. Second, command of the new post was given to Colonel Jir Tramsig, a man disliked by the rank-and-file troops. Tramsig reviewed the troops and ships assigned to his command, made some changes, and brought a smaller force to the system than the military command authorized.

Colonel Tramsig established his first small post on Almas's moon, Dorumaa. From there, he surveyed the situation, attacked a few pirate bases, and eventually brought in more ships. With added troops, he established a larger military base on Cularin itself, erecting a separate platform and building a private military spaceport. Currently, the troop strength in the system consists of two divisions, complete with support units, a fleet of eighteen patrol craft, and four capital warships.

Tramsig's troops actually provide little in the way of police forces, but they do interfere with shipping on a regular basis, usually under the pretense of preventing piracy. The presence is large enough to thwart large-scale raids by pirates, but somehow the pirates always manage to strike just where the patrol routes have the fewest ships.

Colonel Tramsig's strategy is not clear, even to his subordinates. Soon after establishing the base on Cularin, he began requisitioning materials in excess of what his command should need. In addition, he has made deals with Nirama's smugglers for highly questionable technical material. For a man dabbling in so many plans, he doesn't seem to be actually accomplishing much, especially the task he was assigned to accomplish. He's being so overt about his actions that many in the system wonder if he is attempting to hide something that runs much deeper.

Colonel Jir Tramsig

Colonel Tramsig spent the early part of his career doing everything in his power to move through the ranks of the

Republic's military structure. Seen as a promising officer, he nonetheless made some enemies in his rise to power. Mostly successful in battle, he developed a reputation for caring more about the success of his missions than the welfare of the men serving under him. Despite that, he manages to inspire loyalty in his troops. He chooses his own troops carefully, looking for soldiers with the right morals and aggressive attitude to serve under him. Upon his rise to his current rank, he requested an assignment on Cularin. His request was approved immediately. Whether this was because of his abilities or a need to get rid of him remains a subject of speculation and debate.

Tramsig has reddish blond hair he cuts in a very severe style. He wears as many medals on his uniform as he can and dresses to impress his subordinates. He is clean-shaven and has an angular jaw that somehow looks obstinate. He fills out his clothing a little too well, mostly because he wears clothes a few sizes too small, so that the fabric stretches across his body.

Tramsig is a scheming, manipulative man who puts himself first. To succeed, he will hurt anyone who opposes him. The one word that describes him is "cold." He does not needlessly sacrifice others, but he does value life less than other commodities. Tramsig doesn't like anyone. He believes he hides this well, but obviously, he does not. Through heavy-handed means, he and his troops are gaining a bad reputation in the system. He upholds the Republic's interests in the system, but only until they conflict with his own.

Colonel Jir Tramsig: Male Human Soldier 6/Officer 10; Init +3; Defense 20 (+7 class, +3 Dex); Spd 10 m; VP/WP 108/14; Atk +16/+11/+6 melee (2d6, vibroblade), +17/+12/+7 ranged (3d6, blaster pistol); SA Leadership, improved tactics; SV Fort +14, Ref +10, Will +8; SZ M; FP 8; Rep 7; Str 10, Dex 16, Con 14, Int 13, Wis 13, Cha 15.

Skills: Appraise +4, Bluff +9, Computer Use +10, Demolitions +4, Diplomacy +16, Gather Information +6, Intimidate +17, Knowledge (alien species—Tarasin) +9, Knowledge (bureaucracy) +17, Knowledge (Cularin system) +14, Knowledge (galactic politics) +14, Knowledge (culture—military) +16, Pilot +8, Sense Motive +12; Read/Write Basic, Speak Basic, Speak Tarasinese.

Feats: Alertness, Armor Proficiencies (light, medium, heavy), Fame, Iron Will, Persuasive, Point Blank Shot, Weapon Finesse (vibroblade), Weapon Focus (blaster pistol), Weapon Group Proficiencies (blaster pistols, blaster rifles, heavy weapons, simple weapons, vibro weapons).

Yush Baskalar

Baskalar is a severe man whose childhood was disrupted by the Jedi. He was taken from his family for training, only to be discarded because of his penchant for violence. He is Force-Sensitive, but was never trained to use his powers. By the time he returned home, he found that his family was gone. They had left for another system, only to have their

transport destroyed in a terrible accident. Since then, he has harbored a lasting hatred for the Jedi.

The bitter young man had an intense interest in science. His Force talents gave him an edge in studying everything from droid manufacture and cybernetics to the intricacies of Near-Human genetics. He hoped to find a job where he could do specialized research, but unfortunately, his interests were a little too specialized. First, he signed on with a university to do advanced genetics research for the Republic. After he conducted some highly questionable experiments, the university released him. While he was considering what to do next, Qar Jalunn contacted him and offered him unlimited resources to pursue the very experiments that forced his dismissal. He arrived to find his new facilities fully equipped, but unpleasant. He also found that he had to work with the Republic military. The news almost forced him to quit immediately, but Jalunn talked him into staying. He now continues his work on genetics and cybernetics, hating everyone who works with him.

Baskalar is a small Human of middle years with narrow shoulders and a perpetually crooked grimace. He is completely bald, which makes his thin black eyebrows all the more impressive, as they rest on the edge of a slightly prominent superorbital ridge. His back has a slight stoop. While he moves slowly and awkwardly, his hands are impressively nimble. He also has a small, x-shaped scar on his right temple. As a result, he has a developed a tendency to turn the right side of his face away from anyone with whom he's holding a conversation.

Baskalar is short with everyone who might interfere with his work. All of his energies have been focused on his work and his goal of bringing the Jedi to their knees. He speaks with a guttural accent and slurs many of his words. When he is engaged in a conversation with someone who annoys him—that is, just about anyone—his eyelids twitch rapidly.

Yush Baskalar: Male Human Expert 11; Init –1; Defense 12 (+3 class, –1 Dex); Spd 10 m; WP 12; Atk +7/+2 ranged (3d6, blaster pistol); SV Fort +4, Ref +2, Will +7; SZ M; FP 2; Rep 4; Str 10, Dex 9, Con 12, Int 17, Wis 11, Cha 9.

Skills: Computer Use +15, Craft (computers) +11, Craft (droids) +14, Diplomacy +4, Gather Information +13, Knowledge (bureaucracy) +8, Knowledge (physical sciences—chemistry) +13, Knowledge (galactic politics) +6, Knowledge (life sciences—genetics) +16, Repair +9, Search +5; Read/Write Basic, Speak Basic.

Feats: Alertness, Force-Sensitive, Skill Emphasis (Knowledge [genetics]), Skill Emphasis (Craft [droids]), Weapon Group Proficiencies (blaster pistols, simple weapons).

Tira Wils

Tira meandered through life during her early years, eventually joining a mercenary unit. After years of combat, she left the group and took up bounty hunting. She achieved a name for herself and came to the attention of Colonel

Tramsig a year ago. When he moved to the Cularin system, he offered her employment as a special agent. Now she serves as his unofficial chief of security, watching his troops and acting as his bodyguard. Tira is the only member of Tramsig's crew he trusts to deal with the mysterious Qar Jalunn, who occasionally visits. She is also responsible for making sure no one knows about these meetings.

Tira has blue-green skin, snow-white hair, and milky white eyes. Her clothing is skin-tight, and she wears weapons all over her body. Among lowlife scum, she is considered very attractive, but she does not put effort into her appearance beyond trying to look neat. She never smiles.

Only the goals of the moment matter to Tira. For now, they primarily involve protecting Tramsig's interests. She possesses a real devotion to Tramsig, but does not love him—although the question, if ever put to her, might send her into quite a confused state. Truth be known, she is incapable of higher-order emotions. Her senses have been dulled by all the killing she's done. She neither likes nor dislikes anyone. She simply does her job and removes any obstacles that happen to get in her way.

Tira Wils: Female Near-Human Scoundrel 2/Soldier 5/Bounty Hunter 6; Init +8; Defense 26 (+12 class, +4 Dex); Spd 10 m; VP/WP 52/14; Atk +16/+11/+6 melee (2d6, vibroblade), +17/+12/+7 ranged (3d8, heavy blaster); SA Illicit barter, better lucky than good, sneak attack +3d6, target bonus +3; SV Fort +9, Ref +11, Will +6; SZ M; FP 5; Rep 11; Str 16, Dex 18, Con 14, Int 15, Wis 16, Cha 13.

Equipment: Heavy blaster, spare power packs, vibroblade, Z-95 Headhunter.

Skills: Astrogate +5, Climb +10, Computer Use +11, Demolitions +13, Disable Device +11, Disguise +10, Escape Artist +10, Gather Information +8, Hide +14, Intimidate +8, Knowledge (streetwise—Cularin system) +7, Listen +11, Move Silently +14, Pilot +7, Repair +8, Search +12, Sense Motive +12, Spot +11, Treat Injury +7; Read/Write Basic, Speak Basic, Speak Jawa, Speak Huttese.

Feats: Alertness, Armor Proficiencies (light, medium, heavy), Improved Initiative, Multishot, Point Blank Shot, Track, Weapon Focus (heavy blaster), Weapon Focus (blaster rifle), Weapon Group Proficiencies (blaster pistols, blaster rifles, heavy weapons, simple weapons, vibro weapons).

Pirates

While not organized, the pirates operating in the asteroid belt influence many other groups in the system. There are at least eight groups of pirates. Each is independent, and the groups have found themselves fighting over the same goals. Business is good, and with the influx of ships, control of key routes through the belt has become very valuable. Early attempts to negotiate an amicable agreement among the pirate leaders failed, surprising no one. However, the brief armistice did allow two of the pirate organizations, the Red

Fury Brotherhood and the Order of Independent Trade, to substantially augment their power. Working with Nirama (who found their machinations vastly amusing), they smuggled personnel and supplies while most of the system's attention was diverted by the talks. Since then, the Brotherhood and the Order have maintained limited control over sections of the belt. The near-constant infighting makes any kind of stability in the pirate organizations, or their holdings, fairly rare. Nirama keeps one eye on them at all times.

The pirate groups generally have a couple of assault shuttles, some small starfighters, and sometimes a Corellian corvette or two. They scavenge parts from captured ships, and sometimes refit those ships to expand their fleets. Their use of smaller vessels for much of their work makes it easier for them to hide in and among the asteroids, waiting for the proper moment to attack and cripple passing ships. The pirates prefer ships loaded with technical supplies and medical gear on their way insystem. They only rarely bother with anything exported from the system. As long as legitimate exporters in the system are profitable, strong opportunities remain. Recent attempts to acquire military-grade hardware have met with surprising success, much to the dismay of legitimate shipping businesses who have been forced to request and finance Republic navy escorts to ensure safe delivery of their own goods.

For the most part, the pirates raid ships on their own. Bribed spies supply them with departure times, arrival times, and scheduled routes. Some of the groups take jobs from the Metatheran Cartel, Nirama, the mysterious Qar Jalunn, or even Colonel Tramsig. These arrangements are usually brief, and the pirates eventually return to their usual ways. In the Cularin system, the pirates represent a chaotic force, disrupting trade and causing problems. It is relatively unlikely that they will succeed in organizing and forming a united front—too much distrust exists across groups such as the Brotherhood and the Order—but their numbers are troubling. It has been said that Nirama plots to eliminate key members of both the Order and the Brotherhood to "put them in their place." Both groups, however, have their own ideas about Nirama's role in the system. Neither would be particularly upset if he were removed from their affairs. Fortunately for Nirama, internal instability plagues the pirate groups, with assassinations being the preferred means of advancement. Thus, none of the groups keep a solid core of leadership long enough to push any scheme against him beyond the planning stage.

Mysterious Places

Every system has mysterious places. Foolhardy heroes rush to see them, but few return. The ones who survive return with fabulous stories of wealth, power, and danger. Cautious listeners learn of the galaxy's dangers and decide to stay at home. Imaginative ones pass on what they've heard and

embellish it. By adding to the legends, they encourage new generations of heroes to set out and explore. Cularin has more than its share of strange and dangerous places, each with its own mysterious legends.

Cularin: The Ishkik Caverns

When the first platform cities were erected, a group of investors decided to build one in a great valley. The clearing had few trees, mostly rocks and small plants, and was considered ideal for supporting the weight of a large city. This proved to be incorrect. The first column for the city broke through the unexpectedly thin ground and exposed a series of caves. The builders found nothing there except inconvenience. Without exploring what they had found, they chose a new spot for the column and broke through again. A third breakthrough was enough to convince them to move the city to a more stable location farther away.

In the meantime, a group of geologists and scouts explored the caverns, discovering passages that extended for many kilometers. Below the valley, shorter tunnels twisted and turned on each other, but longer passages led to the mountains some distance away. After a cursory exploration, the Humans left. The Tarasin didn't explore the caves until the Tarasin Revolt. During that uncertain time, the caves became home to three irstats of Tarasin. Hidden throughout the tunnels, Tarasin stored blasters, explosives, droids, and vehicles. When the conflict ended, much of the stored material was removed to Gadrin or sold back to offworlders, but some older pieces remained hidden away in clefts and down small side passages.

The stone of the cave resembles granite, but it is not nearly as hard. It's more brittle, and pieces of it fall irregularly as time passes. It is not at all unusual to find a wall section sheared off as if someone cut it down with a mining tool. Tarasin sometimes use the stone as decoration or as material for tools.

No one has really ever explored the full extent of the caves. They are a favorite topic of stories, though, especially in the platform cities of Cularin. The number of people with stories about experiences in the caves is surprisingly high. If you listened to them all, you'd think that the caves were packed full of beings. The stories range from the merely eerie to the hardly believable. Tales include strange new kinds of kilassin, stores of precious crystals and wealth, and even underground cities populated by pale, bulbous humanoids. When questioned on the details, these story-tellers never agree, even when they supposedly witnessed the same events.

Cularin: The Sacred Ch'hala Tree Grove

From the logbook of Reidi Artom:

"The Tarasin took me to a grove of wondrous trees. They were green with purplish bark, producing swirling ripples of color, seemingly at random. The color patterns were similar to the ones the Tarasin create on their scales, but the colors would flow through the trees and fade away, like ripples of water on a lake. The grove had about forty of these trees. In the center, the Tarasin had erected a kind of altar or monument. They said they did not worship there, but instead set up the monument as a celebration of life in the forest."

The "sacred" ch'hala grove is one of the more interesting, and least visited, places on Cularin. Such a sight would attract tourists and scientists by the thousands, but the Tarasin treat the trees as sacred objects and do not allow anyone to witness them without a Tarasin escort. The grove is located more than a thousand kilometers from the nearest platform city, deep in a valley between two small mountain ridges. The forty-two oldest trees of the grove have been growing here for almost three hundred years. The grove is slightly larger than it was during Artom's time: Twenty-eight newer trees have grown there over the last century. The older ch'hala trees have pronounced, elaborate, slowly swirling color patterns. The younger trees have fewer colors and do not glow as brightly, and their patterns change quickly.

The Tarasin placed the stone in the center long before the grove grew around it. The stone commemorates a time in the Tarasin's history when they first began living in irstats. The first two irstats met here and decided that each would live separately. They remained within a day's journey of each other, but far enough apart that each could find sufficient food. The stone marks the point midway between the two village sites. Irstat-kes of the tribes would come to the stone to talk, exchange stories, and evaluate whether tribal existence was better than living as smaller roaming families. Tarasin oral tradition describes this time with reluctant respect, an attitude that characterized the early irstat way of life.

Jedi occasionally come to this grove to meditate when they are in great distress. The swirling patterns on the trees can be calming, almost hypnotic. The Force is as strong here as anywhere else on the planet, but the isolation of the grove helps Jedi focus. Tarasin religious leaders must make a journey to this place once in their lives, bringing back a cutting from one of the trees so that a ch'hala tree can be planted near their irstat's home.

Rennokk: The Cave City

From the logbook of Reidi Artom:

"The molten moon of Cularin has tall spirelike mountains rising from the sea of lava. I am bringing the ship down on the tallest of them. This is my second visit to this place, and I hope to be able to get lower using the pressure suit I brought. The heat disrupted my ship's systems when I tried this last time. . . .

"The pressure suit is working, but it's still very hot. I've left the ship at a cave mouth three kilometers above, and I'm following a cavern tunnel down into the spire. I've reached a junction. The passage leading farther downward is much wider and matches the one I've been using so far. The smaller one leads somewhere on this level. It's different somehow. If I were in a civilized place, I'd say it was used more often. That's just an impression, but it looks like I'll see what's down here before resuming the trek. . . .

"I've been going steadily around in a big circle for the last hour, and don't feel like I've gotten anywhere. I can't find the main vertical tunnel again. I've seen small alcoves in this tunnel, and it looks like the stone was melted away when they were formed. . . .

"Up ahead there's a cave of some kind. Wait, there's something coming toward me. It's large and red and glowing. My sensors say it's incredibly hot. Time to get out of here. . . .

"I've lost it, somehow. I haven't run so hard in my life. Whatever that was, it was alive. It also seems to have been guarding something, considering how fast it came after me. It couldn't have wanted to eat me, since there aren't any Humans on this moon. I may have to come back here with some more firepower and see what I can find out."

Reidi Artom never returned to Rennokk, but a group of explorers did some hundred years after she departed the system. They made their way to the long circular passage and followed it to the end. One being survived, a Tarasin named Kum'Jushkin. According to his report, the group reached the cavern and found the remains of a settlement, all made of metal. The buildings were all connected. Massive structures nearby looked like power generators. Then the lava worm came after them, and the explorers fled. One by one, the members of the group died. Kum'Jushkin said that he was lifting the ship off the planet as the worm reared out of the hole and took a piece out of the ventral stabilizer.

Kum'Jushkin told this story many times, often while he was very drunk. Eventually his embellishments added more and more to the metal city, including the shadows of residents. No one really knows how much to believe anymore, or even if there was a city at all. The damage to his ship and the loss of his companions could be blamed on his own incompetence, or on some accident. The risks of finding out the truth seem out of proportion to its value. Whatever else can be found in the cave, there's some kind of molten monster there no one knows anything about.

Tilnes: Kaernor's Smile

From Kaernor's Story, a well-known tale with an obvious moral:

"Kaernor Belasstie never had much use for conventional wisdom. With an easy laugh, a ready smile, and an oily handshake that revealed much more than the expression on his face, he turned friends into associates and associates into enemies with lightning speed. A latecomer to the mining boom on Tilnes, he heard rumors while drinking in the Underground, stories about untapped resources on the far side that no one wanted to confirm. Travelers spoke of a

53

deep chasm that stretched across most of the moon's face when the suns' light fell on it, one with the potential to produce many easily mined crystals. He couldn't resist. The promise of easy money always lured him, but this time it lured him too far.

"The mining rights to the chasm were easy to come by. Though the files on the area were thick, no one had kept the rights for more than a month or two, and no crystals had ever been extracted from the chasm. It had to be brimming with wealth! How much simpler could it be?

"It proved anything *but* simple. Supplies, he could purchase. Ships, he could purchase. But he couldn't get a crew to sign on with him. Not to go there. His famous smile proved insufficient to convince even the most desperate laborers to accompany him.

"So Kaernor loaded a small shuttle and set out on his own. He took enough gear to harvest a good supply of crystals, hoping to prove it could be done. He grumbled as he loaded the shuttle, and grumbled over his comlink all the way there. Then the comlink went dead.

"The shuttle was never found. Other miners speculated that he went down in the chasm, but no one bothered to go check. His disappearance only reaffirmed what they already knew. They named Kaernor's Smile after him. Things that look easy or attractive from the outside may hide dark secrets we're better off not knowing."

When viewed from above, Tilnes has a distinct pattern on its surface. Near the line where light meets shadow, the line beyond which nothing grows on the planet, a jagged, gaping crevasse stretches for nearly forty kilometers. It's two kilometers wide at its center and tapers to a width of 100 meters at either end before it terminates in a pair of craters. Kaernor's Smile, as it has come to be called, is a place where nothing grows or lives. Those few explorers who have ventured inside have never come out again.

Individuals who have chosen to live on Tilnes avoid Kaernor's Smile as though their lives depended on it. In some sense, they may. The place feels subtly wrong. Tainted. Unclean.

Individuals who travel near Kaernor's Smile report nightmares, vivid dreams of violence and death. The visions never involve people they know. Armies of strangers converge, stabbing or beating each other with primitive weapons. Dark figures always stand in the background. With great flourishes, the dark figures direct the fighting, sending men and women alike to their deaths. Bodies pile toward the sky. Carrion-eaters crawl from holes in the ground. The fighting goes on. And then the dark figures spot the dreamer watching from a distance. They turn. They wave their hands. Then their armies turn as one and start toward the dreamer.

Waking from this dream, the same dream everyone has after going near Kaernor's Smile, is almost as traumatic as the dream itself. Sleeping on Tilnes requires an artificial

night—sleeping masks are popular. Because beings don't always sleep during the same time periods, nightmares can strike at any time. Awake and panicked, many dreamers rise screaming from their beds and run for their lives. Some make it as far as the street before they're tackled and held down. At that point, they usually calm down. Everyone around them knows what the troublesome dream must have been.

Kaernor's Smile is over a kilometer straight down. The narrow chasm cannot be negotiated with shuttlecraft of any kind. The walls of Kaernor's Smile contain small but concentrated deposits of minerals that suck energy from the air around them. Any ship that enters Kaernor's Smile immediately loses power and plummets to the rocks below. No known shields protect against the energy draining power of the minerals, and no sensors can penetrate the vast static field generated within Kaernor's Smile itself.

Theories of Kaernor's Smile's power are varied. Some suggest that the shared dreams are nothing more than mass delusions, people believing in the power of something so much that it becomes real for them. The dreams have been thoroughly documented for generations. They have become part of the culture, so it isn't surprising that many residents have similar dream experiences.

Others believe Kaernor's Smile was imbued, long ago, with a strong dark side influence. The chills they get when they approach Kaernor's Smile could be attributed to the power of the dark side. The Jedi agree that there is some evil presence there, but they do not sense the strong dark side taint so clearly present at the ancient fortress on Almas.

Still others believe that Kaernor's Smile is home to an ancient creature lying in wait for unsuspecting travelers, perhaps a creature that arrived in one of the asteroids that made the craters. To date, no one has mounted an expedition capable of exploring and mapping Kaernor's Smile. Caves within caves, and crevasses within crevasses, hide a secret too dangerous to be known.

Genarius: The Abandoned City of Nub Saar

As floating cities go, Nub Saar wasn't particularly impressive. The small city had half a dozen spires designed to extract samples from the gas-rich atmosphere of Genarius. Nub Saar only had one claim to prominence: its status as the first city built in Genarius's clouds. From a distance, it did little to draw the eye besides breaking up the blue and orange streams that ran through the sky.

Its administrator, a severe Trandoshan named Russok, pushed the construction through its final stages with an almost fanatical fervor. The city stood, silent and ready for occupancy, two months after construction started. In another two months, it would be silent once more.

Russok initially recruited about four thousand five hundred men, women, and children to come to Nub Saar, promising great rewards. "Unlimited potential." "Easy promotions." "Lots of credits." Russok promised whatever it took to draw people, confident that he could not be wrong. He'd seen the initial scans of the atmosphere, and knew how much money could be made.

Then the storms came.

The first storm was the mildest. It ripped the tops off two spires and gave every person in the city radiation sickness for almost a week. Half of the workers left, taking all of the children with them. Only two thousand men remained with Russok. The next storm brought radioactive winds from the planet's core at full force, buffeting the city and peeling metal from the walls, but the storm only lasted half an hour. Seventeen men died from radiation exposure. Another thousand left, and Russok cursed them as their shuttles departed. Then he incinerated the dead bodies.

Three days later, a storm whipped out from the planet's core and engulfed Nub Saar in a swirling, pulsing red and black mist. When the mist cleared, sensors picked up no signs of life. Scout shuttles were dispatched to the city from an orbiting station. The reports that came back sounded like nightmares.

Only the skeletons of the spires remained standing, their steel polished like silvered glass by the radioactive winds. The walls of the spires, and all the other buildings in the city, had been reduced to metallic sludge clogging the streets. There were no signs of the city's inhabitants.

Workers on Genarius have taken the lessons of Nub Saar to heart. The city was left floating in the atmosphere, remaining as a mute reminder of what could happen to any city on the planet. A small floating monument orbits the deserted site, inscribed with the names of the individuals who were lost when Nub Saar was destroyed by strange winds.

It is rumored that the sewer and ventilation systems below the city offered sanctuary. The city was rebuilt with enough supplies in the vast holds below to accommodate 20,000 people and their families. It is not outside the realm of possibility, though extremely unlikely, that some hardy souls survived.

Those who worked on the construction of Nub Saar believe the radiation from the storms is so intense that instruments designed to detect lifeform readings will not work there, especially given the nature of the metals used. From time to time, strange events still occur there. Things appear and disappear from the streets, and some have even reported messages scratched in the dried sludge, only to be smoothed over once more by the next bout of storms. With radiation levels as they are, these stories are dismissed as myths. But still, people wonder . . . .

Eskaron: The Worm
From a story told by Likk Nibk, a spacer and occasional smuggler:

"The modified YT-1300 raced ahead of me through the tunnels, barely turning in time to keep its dish. My Z-95 took the passage with no problem, and I hit full throttle to make my move. The section of tunnel we were heading for

was tricky, and I knew that Riboga was counting on me to beat that YT. If I didn't, I'd find myself floating in space pretty quickly. Easing up a little, I threw myself into the next turn and ducked below the freighter to pass. Problem was, I forgot the tunnel turned upward. The freighter flew into the right passage, and I was forced into a smaller side tunnel. I braked, but couldn't make the turn. The tunnel was just too narrow.

"Just about the time I got the old Z-95 slowed enough to try turning it around, I saw some kind of old cloth or leather hanging in the tunnel ahead. I scanned past it and found that it was part of something that went on for about 100 meters, then stopped. The wall beyond was thin, so I boosted the engines and flew through the structure. I was only in it for a few seconds, but it was strange. It had ridges inside, and some kind of dried goo covered the walls and floor of the passage. The old leather-looking stuff covered the whole tunnel.

"I blasted the rock at the end of the section, broke through to the race course, and shot out just ahead of the YT-1300. Won the race too, which was good for me. When I had time to think about it, I realized that I'd flown through some kind of huge worm creature, sure as I'm standing here telling you about it."

That pilot discovered the only remnant of the space worms that made Eskaron what it is today. The worm's body looks like a stone passage from the inside, but with dried skin covering the whole interior. Any internal organs have long since dried, dissolved, or otherwise disappeared. The segmented parts of the worm are marked by ridges of cartilage, or perhaps just thin stone or calcium deposits. Scientists who have studied the remains say that it's been there for more than 12,000 standard years.

The worm's body is more of a curiosity than anything else. The race course has been altered so that the corpse cannot be used as a short-cut. Scientists studying the worm's remains did not want to be bothered by ships flying through. It now sees little traffic.

Asteroids: The Crystal Snare
From the logbook of Reidi Artom:

"The outer planet of the system is just beyond the asteroid belt, and this is my first visit. The asteroids all read as pretty large, most being several kilometers across. It shouldn't be to hard finding a course through them, though. . . .

"My sensors have locked onto something in the asteroid belt, a large crystal structure. Probably one of the asteroids is filled with crystals, if not several. I'll go take a look. . . .

"I've lost control of the ship. Something near that large crystal reading is overriding my ship systems. Sensors show a transmission of some kind, broadband, and not directed specifically at me. But the ship has turned toward the source, and I can't disengage the computers. Manual controls won't respond. . . .

"I can see the crystal source now. Wow. That whole asteroid is covered with crystal structures. Just as I thought. Sensors say the crystals are not that valuable, but the sight sure is impressive. I'm still piloting right at it, but it's still a few hundred kilometers away, so I can spare the time for a more detailed scan.

"There's some kind of energy pattern beyond the crystal asteroid. I can barely make it out. It seems almost cloaked. It's certainly not natural, at least not in my experience. I'd better do something to get myself out of here. . . .

"Computers are still locked out, so I'm pulling the plug on them. Complete manual piloting feels like the old days. I hope there's enough time. There, the controls are starting to respond. They're sluggish, but responding. . . .

"That was close. As I turned, it looked like the crystals got brighter, as if they were trying to keep me from getting away. I don't have any readings anymore, and of course without this datapad I wouldn't even have the log. I think with more preparation I'll come find this asteroid again and see what its story is. Meanwhile, off to the fourth planet."

Reidi Artom explored this strange site twice more before leaving the system, but never did discover the cause of her first experience. Other scouts and a couple of smugglers have arrived to explore, but three of their ships have disappeared without a trace.

The crystal asteroid is about four kilometers in diameter, roughly spherical, with crystalline structures sticking out from all sides. The crystals are mainly low-grade types used in industry, easily available elsewhere. Some planetologists theorize that the planet from which the asteroid belt was formed had large crystal deposits, and this is the remnant of one of them. That explanation is in fact true, but the asteroid is more than a geological relic.

The asteroid has numerous large crystal shafts running through its length, opening on both sides. The shafts have a gridlike pattern, resembling a large crystal structure of its own. Each shaft is a few meters in width, though two are large enough for a rancor to crawl through. The structure of the shafts, combined with the properties of the crystals themselves, causes the whole asteroid to amplify any transmission sent toward it, including sunlight. Most of the time it sparkles like a tiny star in the sky, reflecting the light from one of the suns. Sensor scans always cause some kind of feedback. It is suspected that blaster fire at the asteroid would reflect in some other direction with more power, but no one has determined a use for this phenomenon, and no one has been able to reproduce it.

The effect on electromagnetic transmissions is thought to explain the energy patterns around the asteroid that Reidi Artom noted in her first visit, but no explorer visiting the site after her first visit, including Artom herself, has seen a repeat

of the patterns. What caused them remains a mystery.

The asteroid receives occasional visits from smugglers wanting to hide from patrol ships, or from the curious. People know not to rely on computers or droids for navigation within a thousand kilometers of the asteroid, though real problems don't begin until a ship is less than 600 kilometers from it. Getting to it is safe once the pilot switches to manual systems, but larger ships, such as military vessels, cannot approach closer than a thousand kilometers safely. For this reason, it's a favorite hideout for smugglers.

Almas: The Fortress of the Sith

From the logbook of Reidi Artom:

"Circling over the fourth planet, I am coming toward a devastated wasteland. A few greenish-purple plants grow here, but that's it. In the center, part of a building protrudes from the ground. The exposed portion is about 30 meters tall with a dome on the top. Sensors say there's more of the structure below the ground. There's something strange about the place. I can feel it, even from here. A Jedi would say that the Force is strong in this place. I don't know about that, but it sure is creepy. The green-purple grasses don't grow anywhere near it.

"The structure is made from some kind of stone, all black. There aren't any entrances or windows of any kind as far as I can see. Sensors cannot penetrate the interior. Whatever it is, someone else is going to have to find out. I'm going to follow a hunch and not land."

The Jedi have records of an ancient Sith Master who used this fortress in his war against the Republic. The building was abandoned, but the stone withstood tremendous amounts of laser fire, and so was left untouched. Since then, only one man has approached closer than a thousand kilometers: Kibh Jeen, a Jedi who eventually turned to the dark side. Since then, no one has wanted to explore the ancient place of evil up close, not even the Jedi.

The exposed portion of the building has no entrances, leaving one to conclude that either the entrance is buried beneath the ground, or the Sith who created it did not need doorways to pass through the rock. Kaluthin used to grow around the site when Artom first explored it, but no longer. The air around it is cold and poisonous. Visitors who approach begin to feel something strange from more than two thousand kilometers away. The wasteland actually reaches much farther. The feeling grows stronger as one approaches the walls. The disturbance is nearly unbearable to anyone not trained in the Force. Jedi have theorized that there is some kind of Force power at work. The threat of the place, more than anything that might actually be present, keeps all but the hardiest from even thinking about going there.

The Almas Academy

The Jedi school on Almas is an experiment of sorts. The Jedi Council watches the school closely, and occasionally sends Jedi to instruct students. The need to teach more Jedi is great, but the Council worries that those not properly chosen and trained will turn to the dark side and pose a threat to the galaxy. The presence of the ancient Sith fortress on the same world also fills some Jedi with concern, but the site was chosen specifically to monitor that taint. As Yoda says, "Hard to see, the dark side is." That being the case, Jedi Master Nerra Ziveri reasoned that the best place to study it would be close by, and that it would prove a constant reminder to the students of the dangers of giving in to fear, aggression, or hate. So far, he has been proven right.

Once established, the Almas Academy grew rapidly. The Tarasin of Cularin began sending children there, and other hopeful candidates followed. Ziveri saw the sudden growth as the will of the Force. In a few exceptional cases, the academy began taking older applicants as well. The academy does not accept applicants the Coruscant temple has already rejected, but some young Tarasin have begun their training when almost adults. A few promising Wookiees and Twi'leks have been brought in during their teen years. These older students have been carefully screened and watched to determine whether they might turn to the dark side, but none have so far. Other than the age differences, the academy uses the same tests to evaluate students as does the Jedi temple on Coruscant. The Almas Academy presents students to the Jedi Council for approval every standard year.

The original academy building was a large circular structure of the same architectural model as the Jedi temple on Coruscant, though on a smaller scale. As the decades passed, additional buildings were added. This building proved to be inadequate once the Tarasin started applying for training. Eight three-story rectagular buildings now surround the original circular temple. The new structures form an octagon and are connected by sealed walkways. Each new structure also connects to the central temple. Thus, the entire complex is sealed against the outside atmosphere. In the "inner court" area, contemplative gardens have been arranged using stone, sand, and the ever-present kaluthin.

The central building holds kitchens, classrooms, and the place of trials. The outer buildings hold the residences of Jedi Knights and Jedi Masters at the school, along with student dormitories. The youngest students live in the same section. The dormitories are organized according to age groups, proceeding clockwise around the octagon. Over the years, as a student grows older, he is moved from section to section.

Many guest chambers and parlors have been included in the design, so that anyone visiting can be accommodated. Additional learning areas have been added to the octagonal sections, including some areas where aspiring Jedi can learn

skills not directly related to the Force. "A Jedi should know as much as possible about everything," says Master Qel-Bertuk.

Curriculum

The original curriculum for Jedi students mirrored that of the Coruscant temple, but as the years progressed, Master Ziveri and Master Qel-Bertuk modified the established methods of teaching to suit the needs of this unusual environment. One big difference between the Coruscant temple and the Almas Academy is the number of Jedi students available. The academy has never had as many applicants as has the temple on Coruscant, but the number of students slowly increases every year. Thus, Master Ziveri has extended the time a student remains within the group learning environment.

In the Cularin system, all of the masters spend time teaching the youngest students (that is, those who have not yet become 1st-level Jedi). Eventually, the young students become Padawan learners (attaining the equivalent of 1st level). They are then assigned to mentors for the duration of their stay at the academy. At that point, students are allowed to travel outside the academy and interact with the system's inhabitants. When a student graduates (becoming a 3rd-level Jedi), he may decide whether to continue his studies at the school or apprentice with a mentor from outside the academy.

The somewhat closed environment of the system also required some changes in training. Normally, Jedi travel the galaxy with their mentors, experiencing a variety of cultures. Tarasin students, on the other hand, strongly object to leaving the system. Most resident instructors are willing to accommodate this desire. Despite the taint of the dark side spreading across the far side of the planet, they prefer the planet's isolation. The remote location has attracted many Jedi who prefer introspection and meditation to adventure and danger. Combined with the closed environment, this makes the academy feel like a monastery.

Because exposure to cultures is necessary and valuable, Master Ziveri sought compromise by expanding the hologram courses on alien culture and instituting the concept of "Jedi quests." During a young Jedi's training at the school, he or she is required to leave the system three times to quest for something that either Master Qel-Bertuk or the student's own mentor requires. The quests began as simple excursions to Coruscant, Corellia, or even Kashyyyk. Soon thereafter, as the masters saw beneficial changes in their students, the quests became more complex. Errands to Hutt Space, the Corporate Sector, and the Core Worlds became popular, and the length of the quests increased.

Most quests begin as simple errands, but the Jedi, meditating on the Force, choose destinations that put the students through more complex experiences than they were expecting. Depending on the destination and possible dangers, the master may accompany the apprentice on this

quest. A Jedi student generally accomplishes one quest per standard year after reaching age 12. Padawans who remain at the academy after graduation (that is, after third level) must undertake one quest every year, and must take a younger student along as well. As a result, the youngest students usually do not have to undertake quests alone unless they choose to do so.

A third peculiarity of the academy's training is the annual Ritual Tale of Kibh Jeen. The Jedi Kibh Jeen was responsible for the academy's presence in a way, since he caused the Dark Jedi Conflict. Cularin's Jedi Masters use his story as a strong warning against the temptation of the dark side, as well as a cautionary tale about exploring the fortress on the far side of the planet. At first, Master Ziveri told the tale every standard year, but he eventually instituted the practice of having the oldest students tell the tale instead. Later, the older students began to reenact the story as a drama for the younger students. One of the masters would always play Kibh Jeen. Through this drama, the younger students were exposed to the story in powerful ways, and the older students learned more complex uses of the Force. In years when there are many older students, they form groups and make the Ritual Tale a competition. Each team tries to tell the story with as much drama, meaning, and insight as possible. The competition is friendly, and no one forgets why the story must be told.

Personalities of the School

The following five characters are the most important figures at the academy.

Lanius Qel-Bertuk

Lanius, the Jedi Master in charge of the academy, is a middle-aged man with smile lines around his eyes. His friendly face sports a salt-and-pepper mustache, as well as a burn scar on his left cheek. He has ice-blue eyes and raven-black hair, and is missing the third finger of his left hand.

As a young student, he arrived at the Jedi temple on Coruscant full of dreams of what he would achieve. Most of these notions had been fueled by popular stories. He found, as most Jedi do, that reality differs greatly from the legends. Finding that he favored the knowledge-based Force arts, he pursued the path of diplomacy. His life took a different turn when his master, the Twi'lek Jedi Nerra Ziveri, took him to Almas to build a new Jedi school. This exposure showed him his talent for teaching students, and he quickly became one of the best-liked instructors at the new academy. During this time, he also learned more about using the Force to probe the future. Yoda once commented on his strong discernment ability when visiting the academy. When Ziveri left the system, Lanius took his place as headmaster, as well as being the chief observer of the Sith fortress on the other side of the planet.

Lanius is friendly, if distant. He has a phenomenal memory, greeting by name every Jedi visiting, attending, or returning to the academy. He does not look people in the face; instead, he wanders around while absently tugging at his beard or muttering. His mind remains sharp, but he cannot focus because of constant distractions from the disturbances he senses. Some have begun to wonder if he is mentally stable. He is, but he also has a strong alliance with the Force. He sensed the disturbance a year before it became noticeable to anyone else, and it continues to distract him.

Because of the disturbances, he has spent more and more time in his meditation chambers trying to see clearly. As a result, his students have suffered. He knows this and feels guilt, but he also senses that finding the source of the disturbance is a greater calling.

Lanius Qel-Bertuk: Male Human Jedi Consular 14; Init +3; Defense 21 (+8 class, +3 Dex); Spd 10 m; VP/WP 84/12; Atk +14/+9 melee (4d8+2, lightsaber); SA Healing; SV Fort +10, Ref +9, Will +12; SZ M; FP 16; Rep 19; Str 14, Dex 16, Con 12, Int 16, Wis 17, Cha 17.

  Equipment: Lightsaber.

  Skills: Diplomacy +20, Knowledge (Cularin system) +13, Profession (educator) +20, Sense Motive +10; Read/Write Basic, Speak Basic, Speak Tarasinese, Speak Hutt.

  Force Skills: Affect Mind +11, Empathy +11, Enhance Senses +14, Farseeing +20, Force Defense +9, Force Push +8, Friendship +11, Heal Self +9, Move Object +11, See Force +16, Telepathy +20.

  Feats: Exotic Weapon Proficiency (lightsaber), Skill Emphasis (Profession [educator]), Trustworthy, Weapon Finesse (lightsaber), Weapon Group Proficiencies (blaster pistols, simple weapons).

  Force Feats: Alter, Burst of Speed, Control, Deflect Blasters, Dissipate Energy, Force Mastery, Force-Sensitive, High Force Mastery, Sense.

E1-6RA

As a droid administrator of the Jedi Academy, E1 was purposely constructed with parts from as many different droids as possible, giving her a unique appearance. Her basic frame is that of a protocol droid, but she has four arms, two of which extend from just above her waist and terminate in tool mounts. She carries a variety of small tools to mount on these extra limbs. Her plating is bronze-colored with some permanent blaster scoring.

Internally, she sports a heuristic processor, which allows her to learn, and a piece of alien technology that receives telepathic transmissions, translating them into signals she can understand. This piece of technology comes from beyond the Outer Rim. It was installed into E1 on a whim by a smuggler who wanted to hide it from the authorities. Since he was arrested anyway, the module remained installed in E1. She passed through many masters and was modified many times before Lanius found her. He bought her from the family of a new student and brought her to Culria some years ago. Lanius calls her Era, but students must refer to her as E1-6, or "EeOne."

Something of an all-purpose droid, E1 is prepared for anything and always willing to do Lanius's bidding. Using her heuristic processor, she learns which new skills may be required and programs herself to handle whatever situation may come up at the academy. Stuffy but not prissy, she expresses herself with stiff speech patterns and convoluted sentences. She was once programmed for replicating humor, but part of that programming was overwritten by more practical software. Thus, she still attempts jokes, but they are nearly always awful. The only person who consistently laughs at them is Lanius. Even then, he responds with a dry, hollow laugh. The students lean toward groans, if they respond at all. Working with Jedi has been the best service she remembers. She is utterly devoted to serving Lanius and the academy.

E1-6RA: Walking droid Expert 9; Init +0; Defense 13 (+3 class); Spd 8 m; WP 12; Atk +6/+1 melee and ranged (no weapons); SV Fort +6, Ref +5, Will +7; SZ M; Rep 5; Str 10, Dex 10, Con 13, Int 16, Wis 12, Cha 8.

   Equipment: Two extra arms with tool mounts, vocabulator, comlink, alien telepathic receiver unit, improved sensor package, heuristic processor, locked access, motion sensors, translator unit (DC 30), recording unit (audio).

   Skills: Computer Use +12, Craft (electronics) +7, Diplomacy +1, Disable Device +11, Gather Information +2, Knowledge (Cularin system) +12, Knowledge (galactic politics) +7, Knowledge (Jedi lore) +12, Knowledge (physical sciences—physics) +7, Listen +7, Repair +11, Search +7, Spot +9, Treat Injury +3; Speak Basic, Speak Tarasinese.

   Feats: Cautious, Great Fortitude, Lightning Reflexes, Sharp-Eyed.

Kirlocca

Kirlocca, a Wookiee Jedi, came to the academy when he was young, but he was already older than most students, even for the Almas Academy. Fortunately, his talent with the Force was strong, and Ziveri accepted him immediately. He was the last pupil Ziveri accepted to the school before he disappeared. Kirlocca, feeling deeply grateful, worked hard to prove himself worthy of Ziveri's trust, even after Ziveri was gone. Pursuing the path of the guardians, Kirlocca became one of the foremost masters of lightsaber technique. His natural Wookiee reflexes and strength, honed by the Force, make him nearly unbeatable. Kirlocca teaches lightsaber technique at the academy. He also helps with basic Force exercises and oversees certain aspects of the Jedi Trials.

   Normally kind-hearted, Kirlocca hides a ferocity that comes out when he fights. Students can expect him to answer questions with simple yet baffling answers or a shake of his furry head. He possesses a great deal of wisdom, but has decided that the best way to impart what he knows is through martial training. He teaches young Jedi to harness their energies through the fluid art of the lightsaber. He does not howl or shriek when he fights; he has long since aban-

doned the Wookiee war cries. Instead, he moves in combat with an eerie silence. He also refuses to draw on his Wookiee rage—he feels that giving in would invite the dark side. A strong Jedi, he will not hesitate to kill anyone who violates what he sees as the will of the Force.

   Kirlocca's coloring is predominately dark, but parts of his face and his arms have lighter brown fur.

Kirlocca: Male Wookiee Jedi Guardian 11; Init +7; Defense 22 (+9 class, +3 Dex); Spd 10 m; VP/WP 110/17; Atk +16/+11/+6 melee (4d8+5, lightsaber); SA Healing; SQ Wookiee rage; SV Fort +10, Ref +10, Will +8; SZ M; FP 12; Rep 8; Str 20, Dex 17, Con 17, Int 14, Wis 17, Cha 10.

   Equipment: Lightsaber.

   Skills: Astrogate +3, Climb +9, Craft (lightsaber) +5, Escape Artist +4, Intimidate +13, Knowledge (Jedi lore) +10, Sense Motive +4, Spot +4, Survival +4, Tumble +10; Speak Shriiwook, Understand Basic.

   Force Skills: Battlemind +9, Enhance Ability +8, Enhance Senses +8, Force Defense +8, Heal Self +5, See Force +9, Telepathy +5.

   Feats: Exotic Weapon Proficiency (lightsaber), Improved Initiative, Weapon Group Proficiencies (blaster pistols, simple weapons).

   Force Feats: Alter, Control, Deflect Blasters, Force-Sensitive, Knight Defense, Lightsaber Defense, Sense, Throw Lightsaber.

Seenlu Kir

Seenlu trained as a consular at the Jedi Temple on Coruscant. Three standard years after becoming a Jedi Knight, she chose to join the academy on Almas. She has trained students at all levels of mastery. Now she leaves the advanced training to other instructors and oversees the dormitory where the youngest students live.

   Seenlu stands nearly 1.6 meters tall. Her brown hair falls down to her waist. Her green eyes look upon the world with compassion and a hint of laughter. She dresses in pants, shirts, and vests instead of the traditional Jedi robes, but her lightsaber still rests at her side. Gloves conceal burns on her hands that she refuses to have treated in bacta. Her scars do not pain her, but they remind her of a failure in her past that she does not care to talk about. Nearing her 40th year, Seenlu has no regrets for the path she has chosen, except that she would like to raise a family of her own. At the academy, she doesn't see that happening, but she knows where she is needed. It is the will of the Force that she should remain at the Almas Academy, so that is where she will stay.

Seenlu Kir: Female Human Jedi Consular 8; Init +2; Defense 18 (+6 class, +2 Dex); Spd 10 m; VP/WP 57/13; Atk +6/+1 melee (3d8, lightsaber); SA Healing; SV Fort +7, Ref +6, Will +8; SZ M; FP 8; Rep 6; Str 11, Dex 15, Con 13, Int 15, Wis 15, Cha 14.

Equipment: Lightsaber.

Skills: Computer Use +7, Diplomacy +10, Knowledge (alien species—Tarasin) +6, Knowledge (Cularin system) +6, Knowledge (Jedi lore) +8, Listen +5, Profession (educator) +6, Sense Motive +8, Treat Injury +10; Read/Write Basic, Speak Basic, Speak Tarasinese.

Force Skills: Empathy +13, Enhance Senses +9, Friendship +9, Heal Another +5, Heal Self +6, See Force +7, Telepathy +6.

Feats: Exotic Weapon Proficiency (lightsaber), Skill Emphasis (Empathy), Trustworthy, Weapon Group Proficiencies (blaster pistols, simple weapons).

Force Feats: Alter, Burst of Speed, Control, Dissipate Energy, Force Mastery, Force-Sensitive, Sense.

"Mother" Missira

When the first Tarasin students entered the Almas Academy, Tarasin elders became concerned that they would find life away from their tribes alarming. Because of this, the elders believed most Tarasin students would fail. Despite the elders' admonitions, students still apply. Missira, one of the Force Adept leaders of the Tarasin religion, was thus chosen to go to the academy and serve as a "Mother" to the Tarasin there. She has gathered them into a separate tribe, easing their transition into the society of the larger galaxy. So far, this strategy has proven very successful.

Missira's duties include overseeing the kitchens. In the past, the academy had an excellent droid chef named O2-C4, but a small group of students accidentally destroyed O2 when their powers got away from them. Missira took over the kitchens and had the droids reprogrammed to obey her. The academy ordered a new droid. Everyone is still waiting for the new cook, but Missira does such a good job with the food that no one really wants it to arrive.

A tall humanoid with regal bearing, Missira is well-suited to her new position as a tribal leader. She would not, under normal circumstances, have achieved the position on Cularin, since she is part of a religious order. She loves children and enjoys the task of teaching them to retain their cultural heritage as they learn to be Jedi. She has a quirky sense of humor, one she developed after leaving Cularin. She tries to understand E1's attempts at humor, but finds them sadly flat. She tries to help, though, and has formed a friendship of sorts with the administrator droid.

Missira: Female Tarasin Force Adept 9; Init +1; Defense 17 (+6 class, +1 Dex); Spd 10 m; VP/WP 59/13; Atk +5/+0 melee (1d6, quarterstaff, see below); SA Force weapon, comprehend speech, Force talisman; SQ +4 species bonus to Survival checks in heat conditions, −2 species penalty to Bluff and Sense Motive checks; SV Fort +5, Ref +5, Will +8; SZ M; FP 9; Rep 4; Str 9, Dex 13, Con 13, Int 16, Wis 15, Cha 11.

Equipment: Force staff (use 3 vitality to get +1d4 damage bonus for 9 rounds); Force talisman (grants +2 Force bonus to saving throws against Force skills and Force feats).

Skills: Hide +5, Knowledge (Cularin system) +15, Craft (cooking) +9, Knowledge (Jedi lore) +7, Sense Motive +6, Spot +10, Survival +10, Treat Injury +7; Speak Basic, Understand silent Tarasin color language.

Force Skills: Affect Mind +12, Enhance Senses +6, Force Defense +10, Force Push +11, Force Stealth +6, Friendship +2, Heal Another +12.

Feats: Endurance, Track, Weapon Group Proficiencies (blaster pistols, primitive weapons, simple weapons).

Force Feats: Alter, Control, Dissipate Energy, Force Mastery, Force-Sensitive, Sense.

Living Force Campaign Information

Star Wars holds a special attraction for many people. In that distant galaxy, epic stories of heroism are played out before our eyes and in our minds. Now, with the new *Star Wars Roleplaying Game,* you have a chance to put yourself into this fantastic setting and tell your own stories of adventure and heroism. Through the RPGA® Network, you can become part of the Living Force campaign and share your *Star Wars* experiences with thousands of gamers around the world.

The RPGA Network

The RPGA Network is an international roleplaying fan club and organized play organization with more than 60,000 members around the world. Branch offices in North America, England, Belgium, and Australia serve members everywhere, and the Network is growing rapidly. RPGA members gather to play roleplaying games, meet others with similar interests, and promote the roleplaying hobby.

RPGA members receive two bimonthly magazines every year. In odd-numbered months, members receive the *Living Greyhawk Journal,* with 32 pages devoted to the world's largest D&D campaign. In even-numbered months, members receive *Polyhedron* magazine, a 64-page global roleplaying magazine. *Polyhedron* features gaming articles and tips for all game systems (including the *Star Wars* game), support articles for the RPGA's Living campaigns, club news, reviews of products, and interviews. Members also receive a professionally designed roleplaying adventure once per year, as well as a chance to playtest upcoming Wizards of the Coast roleplaying products. And as a member, you'll have access to our huge library of roleplaying scenarios for a large variety of game systems. You can order these for conventions, game days, home game play, or use on the Internet.

In the U.S., RPGA membership costs $20 per year in most places. Rates vary outside the U.S.; check with RPGA headquarters for the price where you live. You can join online at www.rpga.com or send a check or money order and a letter

to RPGA Network, *Star Wars* Character Option, P.O. Box 707, Renton WA 98057-0707 USA.

Living Campaigns

One of the RPGA's biggest and most successful programs is the Living campaign program. A Living campaign is like a home campaign, but conducted on a much larger scale. Players make characters according to our guidelines and play them in sanctioned adventures for the campaign. These adventures can be played at conventions, game days, or at home. By participating in a Living campaign, you have the opportunity to interact with thousands of players rather than four to seven, and you can develop your characters as if you were playing at home. Most campaigns have ongoing plot threads, so your character can do the same kinds of heroic deeds that he or she would do in your home game.

Living Force

The Living Force campaign takes place in the *Star Wars* universe one year after the events of *The Phantom Menace*. Political fallout from the Trade Federation's actions on Naboo spreads through the galaxy, and the Republic begins to crumble. The Cularin system has just joined the Republic, but it must also face its own unique problems.

Like the movies, the campaign is story-intensive. Story arcs take place in one-year periods. Each major story consists of three trilogies (three-part adventures), and one to three supplementary adventures. These adventures will be available for conventions before they're available for home game groups. You can play in the main stories of the campaign without leaving your home.

Supplemental campaign information will be released through the RPGA's *Polyhedron* magazine, Wizards of the Coast's *Star Wars Gamer* magazine, and on the RPGA website at www.rpga.com. These sources will provide additional material on the Cularin system and other systems in Living Force stories. The Force will be with us.

Making a Character
Version 1.0 January 2001

To make a Living Force character, you'll need a copy of the *Star Wars Roleplaying Game* core rulebook. The guidelines below describe changes needed for a "living" campaign environment. All Living Force characters must comply with the most current version of the *Star Wars Roleplaying Game* core rules and these guidelines (by version number).

Instead of following the steps outlined below, you may select one of the Fast-Track Character Templates from the main rulebook. The templates are complete characters, so you can select one, name the character, skip to Step 6 below, and start playing. Character templates should not be modified. If you want a character that's slightly different from one of the templates, follow the instructions below instead.

Step 1: Ability Scores

Assign your ability scores using the planned character creation method on page 11 of the *Star Wars Roleplaying Game* rulebook. You can also choose to use the standard score package described on that page. Apply species modifiers to ability points after the base scores are determined. Ability points gained from level advances do not use this chart. At every fourth character level, add one point to any one ability.

Because the Living Force campaign strives for a heroic feel, all characters add one point to any ability at second character level, in addition to the points acquired every fourth character level.

Step 2: Species and Class

Choose a species for your character. The following species are allowed for Living Force characters. Other species are reserved for Gamemaster characters or have not been discovered by the galaxy at large during the time of the campaign.

Star Wars Roleplaying Game rulebook: Human, Cerean, Gungan, Ithorian, Rodian, Sullustan, Trandoshan, Twi'lek, Wookiee.

Living Force Campaign Guide: Tarasin.

Choose any class for your character described in the *Star Wars Roleplaying Game* rulebook.

Prestige Classes: Players may choose the following prestige classes for their characters: bounty hunter, elite trooper, starfighter ace, officer. Characters must qualify for these classes as described in the *Star Wars Roleplaying Game* rulebook.

Multiclass Restriction: In the Living Force campaign, choosing the path of the Jedi requires complete devotion. Jedi consulars and Jedi guardians who add additional classes after taking up the Jedi class can never again advance as a Jedi, though they retain any Jedi class abilities they have earned in the past. If a character has fewer than seven levels in the Jedi class when he or she abandons it, the character loses the lightsaber acquired at the first Jedi class level. It must be returned to the character's master.

Step 3: Vitality Points

Living Force characters receive vitality points at each class level according to the following table. Add Constitution bonuses to the values in this table.

Fringer	6	Soldier	8
Noble	4	Force Adept	6
Scoundrel	4	Jedi Consular	6
Scout	6	Jedi Guardian	8

Step 4: Skills and Feats

Choose skills and feats for your character. The Profession and Craft skills are deliberately open-ended in the game rules, so these specific rules apply:

Profession and Craft skills do not add synergy skill bonuses to any other skill. Furthermore, Profession and Craft skills cannot be used in place of skills described in the *Star Wars Roleplaying Game* rulebook. For example, skill ranks in Profession (starship pilot) or Craft (starship) cannot help you make Pilot or Repair checks.

Profession and Craft skills can be used to generate income for your character. Because the campaign focuses on story elements, we have simplified the means of generating income, and there are rules for generating income between adventures. Profession and Craft skills can help boost your income when using these rules. You cannot use Profession or Craft skills to generate income by other means. Player characters can craft items from the equipment chapter of the *Star Wars Roleplaying Game* rulebook and sell them to other player characters. Characters cannot craft lightsabers (except as detailed below), ships, vehicles, or droids. It is best to derive income from the use of Craft and Profession skills in your character's background, rather than during adventures. (After all, did you see Han, Leia, or Obi-Wan stop in the middle of a movie to make blast armor to sell to their friends?)

Jedi characters (consulars and guardians) must craft their own lightsabers before reaching 7th level. Once the character reaches 6th level in a Jedi class, construction of a Jedi's lightsaber takes place in the background. When a Jedi makes his or her own lightsaber, the old lightsaber is returned to the academy.

Step 5: Equipment

Starting characters receive maximum credits for their class. Characters can purchase equipment listed in the Equipment chapter of the *Star Wars Roleplaying Game* rulebook, with the following exceptions.

The following items are not allowed for player characters: double-bladed lightsabers, stormtrooper armor.

The following items are legally restricted: security toolkits, vibro-axes, heavy blaster pistols, any weapon in the heavy weapons group, and thermal detonators. Possession of this equipment is allowed, but characters cannot buy it through normal channels. Permits for these items may be available in play. Legal penalties will be applied during adventures to characters found possessing these items without proper permits.

Lightsabers are acquired in play or by class choice. They cannot be purchased.

Characters may not purchase vehicles, starships, or droids, except through play opportunities.

Watch how much your gear weighs. We don't usually worry about encumbrance, but if you pack an excessive amount of gear, you will find yourself slowed down.

Step 6: Background

Characters in the Living Force campaign are heroes, not villains. The adventures are centered around heroic experiences. Please do not play villainous characters.

Your character may be of any height or weight allowed for your species. Your character begins at any age between adulthood and old age, as defined in Chapter 6 of the *Star Wars Roleplaying Game* rulebook.

You should determine your character's history up to this point, and you should be able to explain why he or she is in the Cularin system. Character concepts that do not fit this campaign should be avoided.

Special Character Opportunities

Guild-level and Family RPGA members have special options for their characters, as described below. To participate in these options, you must register your character either at an interactive convention event where these opportunities are present, or register online through our character database. If you don't have access to the Web, you can mail a copy of your character and your request to RPGA Network, *Star Wars* Character Option, P.O. Box 707, Renton WA 98057-0707 USA.

The opportunities are described by type, with notations for character classes that can take advantage of each one. Multiclassed characters can take advantage of any options that any of their classes qualify them for, but each player can only make use of one of these options at a time. If a player has generated multiple characters, only one of them can use one of these options at any given time.

These opportunities should be used to encourage roleplaying during adventure play.

Jedi Training

Jedi player characters begin as Padawan learners. Each character is assumed to have a mentor. Until a character becomes a 3rd-level Jedi guardian or consular, his or her mentor is generally assumed to be in the background, training the Padawan between adventures. The mentor can be contacted during adventures, but cannot directly participate. Jedi study as Padawan learners until they reach 7th level.

At the 3rd class level, the Jedi can declare a specific mentor. A Jedi Knight player character may volunteer to mentor the Padawan; otherwise, the Gamemaster plays the mentor. The relationship between the mentor and Padawan must be registered with the campaign staff. A mentor cannot train more than one Padawan.

Force Adept Apprentices

Upon reaching the 3rd class level as a Force adept, a character can attract an apprentice to his or her way of viewing the Force. The apprentice begins as a commoner and adventures with the player character. After five completed adventures in which the Force adept character receives more than fifty percent of the possible experience available per character, the apprentice becomes a 1st-level Force adept. Thereafter, the apprentice acquires experience at the same rate as other characters, but cannot have more than half the class levels that the player character has as a Force adept (rounded down). Thus, a 3rd-level Force adept could have a 1st-level Force adept apprentice. If the same 3rd-level Force adept also had six levels of the scoundrel class, the character could still only have a 1st-level Force adept apprentice. The apprentice only gains levels as a Force adept. Once the apprentice reaches 7th level, he leaves the player character and strikes out on his own.

Regular reports on the apprentice must be submitted to the campaign staff. These reports should be sent when the apprentice reaches 1st level, and whenever the apprentice gains a level. When the apprentice leaves the player character, a full report should be made, so that the apprentice can be integrated into the campaign as a Gamemaster character.

Calling in Exceptional Favors

Noble class characters can call upon favors as a class ability. In the Living Force campaign, certain classes of characters can call upon exceptional favors of different types. All three kinds of favors described below should be governed using the general guidelines for noble favors (as described in the rulebook), with one difference: The DC for a favor should be cut in half.

These favors can be requested by characters of 3rd class level and above. A single character can have one of these favors active at a time. The character must use the favor, and report the use and results to the campaign staff, before receiving another such favor (or any other special character option).

Use of these favors comes with a cost. The first time one of these favors is used, the character does not have to repay it. The second time one is used, the Gamemaster character granting the favor can request a favor in return, which the character must try to fulfill. Such a favor should depend on the context, the Gamemaster granting it, and the nature of the current adventure. The favor that the player character must grant should not be directly related to the adventure; in fact, it can be totally unrelated to the adventure. However, it must be something the character has the ability to grant.

Noble Exceptional Favor (Noble Class Only): Powerful Gamemaster characters in the campaign grant these favors. Examples include the Baron Administrators on Cularin, Nirama (a local crimelord), and Colonel Tramsig.

Scoundrel Illicit Goods Favor (Scoundrel Class Only): This favor is used to acquire a piece of illegal or restricted equipment for use during the adventure. Examples include heavy blaster rifles or thermal detonators for a demolitions or heavy combat mission, special tools for an infiltration mission, or a load of spice for a decoy mission of some kind. Its use should tie to an adventure; the favor cannot be used to enrich the scoundrel character. Whether the character can keep the piece of equipment or not depends on where it came from. In the report on the favor, the player should explain how and why the item was obtained, and the campaign staff will decide whether to certify it or not.

Fringer Extra-System Favor (Fringer Class Only): This favor can accomplish the same things that the noble or scoundrel versions can, but it is granted by the fringer's contact somewhere in the Outer Rim. Because the source is far away, the time elapsed between requesting the favor and receiving it depends on the nature of the favor. Information should take about a day to get back to the fringer, while a piece of equipment may take several days or weeks to be brought insystem.

Ships and Droids

Acquisition of starships, vehicles, and droids is controlled by the campaign staff. Upon reaching 3rd character level, a player may acquire a ship or droid for one of his or her characters. The ship or droid comes with a debt equal to its cost, which must be paid. Regular payments can be made (so a character can get a ship before being able to afford it), or the whole can be paid in a lump sum. If regular payments are not made, then thugs come to collect the credits owed each time the character is played in an adventure. If payments are not made for a long enough period, the ship or droid is confiscated.

Once the ship or droid has been paid for, the character can make improvements (according to the rules presented in the *Star Wars Roleplaying Game* rulebook) at interactive events.

Heroes of the soldier class can purchase classification four droids, those armed and used for military applications. Characters of other classes can only purchase noncombat droids (classifications one, two, three, and five). Droids that are not classification four cannot be equipped with armaments.

Heroes of the scout class acquire their ships through more legitimate means, and therefore do not suffer the risk of visits from thugs. Scouts also get their ships at a discount.